The PASSAGE, The GIFT, And The PROPHECY

Also by Jeff Gutterman

July
Death and Passing Over—The Magical Journey
The Romantic and the Genius
Quirks

The PASSAGE, The GIFT, And The PROPHECY

Jeff Gutterman

SilverWind
PUBLISHING

Cover Photographs by Jeff Gutterman
Cover Photograph of Chris Griscom by Teo Griscom, used with permission
Cover design and illustration by Craig Upton

The publisher wishes to thank Judy Berlinski, and Craig Upton for their professional assistance with the preparation of this book. In addition, a big thank you goes to Allison Ragle, with a very special note of thanks going to Teo and Chris Griscom for their generosity.

SilverWind Publishing, Los Angeles California

Printed in Canada
First Printing: April 2000

Library of Congress Catalog Card Number: 99-093660
ISBN 1-893676-01-3

*For those who are open to different perceptions . . .
adding to their treasure chest of knowing*

Preface

Years ago, in a time all but forgotten, lived a magical old woman. She had chosen long ago to shelter herself in a land in a far off place, nestled high on a mountain on the perimeter of a small valley. Measured by years her life spanned over one-hundred and fifty summers and winters. Vibrant and more alive than any of the people in the valley, she held the key and the riddle to the essence of life itself. Beautifully fair and simple in complexion she reflected all that was magical within her physical surroundings. Much like the trees that surrounded her land, she stood tall and graceful with her long golden hair swaying in the mild winds that kicked up their heels every now and then. Her eyes, soft and soothing, could pull you into her being and comfort you within the cradle of her world. Instinctively you knew this was a world rich and stimulating in all possible ways. Her arms, soft and supple, could embrace you with the energy of love in a way that would quell your innermost emotions. Quick of mind and long on compassion, her advice was sought and respected by all of the valley people.

She was light. And so it was that the valley people called her Tandara, an ancient Sanskrit word for "the enlightened one." As such and in turn, each physical within the valley would at some time make their own pilgrimage to the top of the mountain. Occasionally there were those that would make the journey more than once. But whether once or many times, there always seemed to be an envelope of comfort and trust with the unfamiliar words Tandara would speak to each of them once the decision was made to seek her guidance. One such pilgrim was Cashel, a small physical in most ways, but certainly not in stature. For Cashel was just at that point in life where wonder still ruled her world. Slender and lithe with olive colored skin, her long flowing black hair was matched only by the richest, deepest pools of ebony expressed in her eyes. She was a multicolored sponge absorbing her sur-roundings with every chance she had while remaining open to the wonder of all around her. She reflected the essence of the wild flowers that grew unhindered in the meadow within the valley, just as she mirrored the squirrels that ran wild and free who had become her friends. And she sensed a wonderful abandon of the birds and butterflies she would talk to as they sat perched on a branch or twig surrounded by the framework of their world. Also, there were the other physicals within the valley that she would talk with from time to time, exchanging stories of their unending experiences on life. But most of all, she enjoyed the nonphysicals that were beginning to enter her world each time that she chose to visit Tandara.

Chapter One

They found themselves holding hands at the base of the mountain, eyes closed, stillness and silence lighting their minds, as they both viewed the winding path that made its way to the top. When they opened their eyes and began searching the mountainside, small bits and pieces of the normally invisible artery they needed to locate and travel on became visible to them. But their destination was well out of view, the peak many feet beyond the layer of cloud-covering that surrounded the mountain on all sides.

Dragit was the first to speak. "It's too high and too long. I'm getting tired just looking at it. I don't see why I have to go anyway."

With a sigh that was becoming commonplace to her, Cashel removed her hand from Dragit's. "I've already told you why. Tandara said that on my seventh trip to see her I should bring my younger brother. You're my younger brother. Now stop complaining. It won't take that long to get to the top and you'll really like it once you get there. There's magic all over."

And with that they started their climb. Cashel leading, with Dragit several feet behind her. Half-listening to her brother's continuing comments, Cashel found herself almost floating to Tandara, sensing her excitement when the two would see each other again. Cashel with her childlike wonder and all encompassing innocence, and Tandara with her encouraging words and motions, as though the two were meeting for the first time. She could feel Tandara's arms wrapped around her in a pleasant hello, her hugs pulling the two of them together. Words unnecessary as all time stood still. And it was these thoughts that sustained her as she made her way up the mountain to the plateau that was Tandara's world.

Dragit however, was fighting his journey with every step. "I just don't understand why you want to go see some old woman. There are plenty of old women in the village and you don't have to climb some dumb old mountain to see them."

"Will you please give it a rest. I'm telling you, the climb will be worth it."

Only a few years younger than Cashel, Dragit shared a wonderfully matched complexion, together looking as though they had been held by their feet at birth and dipped into the most delightful vat of deep brown olive sauce. Also identical to Cashel were those incredibly large dark eyes and long black hair. But that's where the similarities appeared to stop, both physically and emotionally. Physically he was both shorter and stockier than Cashel, not by much but enough to distinguish them one from the other. And where Cashel was caught up in the wonder of her new experiences, Dragit was always fighting his in every way he could.

Even though they were now walking over it, most of the winding dirt path that lay ahead of them remained invisible until they were almost on top of it. Viewed from above, the trail that led to the plateau was both steep and pockmarked with a variety of small holes and overgrown brush. On both sides of the path, beginning halfway up the mountain, were lines of fruit trees planted there by Tandara many years ago. They were closely cultivated each season for those visitors that chose to refresh themselves, each as they made their way over the landscape. This year though, as Cashel reached the point where the trees usually began, she noticed many of the branches were empty and barren. There were few leaves left that helped nourish and support the fruit that hung from the branches of the trees. Many had disappeared, taking with them the very fruit itself, and of course, the beauty they represented. Disquieted by a lack of reason or justification, Cashel maintained her ascent to Tandara saying nothing to Dragit of the way the path normally presented itself, but rather reinforcing the image of how beautiful it was the way they were seeing it.

"Isn't this wonderful Dragit? Can you feel the air change as we get higher? It makes me feel so . . . "

"I don't know what's so wonderful about it. I keep falling into these holes. I'm gonna break my leg and you're going to have to carry me up the mountain . . . What? What did you say?"

As Cashel lowered her head, Dragit could barely make out the words, "And I promise not to throw you off of it when we get to the top."

That did it. Now Dragit stopped and took a serious stance and it was soon apparent to Cashel that he wasn't directly behind her. "What's wrong now?"

"How come you climb this mountain so often? And you get so excited every time you do it?"

The Passage, the Gift, and the Prophecy

Cashel slowly turned around and glanced back at Dragit. "I climb the mountain to see Tandara because I learn something new every time I see her. Besides, this time she has a gift for me."

"What kind of a gift?"

"I don't know. But it doesn't matter. I enjoy seeing her and my other friends even without a gift."

"What other friends?"

"Dragit, I've told you four times already. You're making me nuts . . . Alright. Once again. I get to see Palimar and Ginruss."

"Why don't they come down to see you?"

"Dragit, I'm going to turn around and continue climbing. If you want to come with me you can. There's something on the mountaintop for you also, or Tandara wouldn't have invited you." And with that Cashel turned and made good on her promise.

On the other side of the mountain, well out of view of the path Cashel and Dragit were on, was yet a second path. Equally as steep, equally marked with holes and underbrush, and just as equally lined with fruit trees. But unlike Cashel's eye view of an almost barren landscape, these trees contained all the missing leaves and fruit that helped enhance and sustain the climb to

Tandara. This passageway, though, had no pilgrim upon its back.

The third pathway leading to Tandara was also found to begin at the base of the mountain. But it was different than the other two. The surface of the road was neither pockmarked with minor impressions nor lined with brush or trees of any kind. Instead, the warm watery pass was in fact a stream that flowed in an upward direction. Barely several feet deep, it gave the impression of a calm, silken-like escalated river, that moved and made its way toward the impressionable blue sky with little effort. Winding and forging a circular course around the mountain, as though gaining ever increasing strength with each circumference, it made its way toward its source. This indeed was the most beautiful path. Its differences though were significant, including its ability to remain invisible from most eyes.

One pair of eyes that had noticed its beauty and strength belonged to an old man. Quiet in appearance, he stood just straight enough to blend in nicely with his surroundings. His eyes were crystal-like, reflecting his feelings of completeness and his joy for life. His skin was tanned yet soft, deeply enhanced by his thick white hair and grayish white midlength beard. Like Tandara he was tall, but unlike her, settled somewhere between slender and strong-boned. He was quite a magnificent sight.

With his words to the winds, his voice deep and mellow, carried beyond the space that surrounded him. "Tandara my old friend and teacher. It's been several years since I've seen you. You've surely been missed. I look forward to seeing your smiling face again. For whatever reason you've called me."

And just as Cashel and Dragit made their way to the top of the mountain on their path, through their ability and knowledge that forward movement comes by putting one foot in front of the other, the old man began his journey by gently laying down on top of the velvet-like stream, and allowing its upward motion to carry him to the top of the mountain.

The grounds of the plateau were spacious, more so than the most vivid imagination would allow. Seen from the bottom of the mountain, the ridge of the plateau looked uninvitingly small. But as each Ascension was made, from whatever path had been chosen by those seeking Tandara, the ridge became increasingly intimidating by its size. Once on top, the idea of a small space receded to the back of your mind immediately. Covered mostly by a rolling light green grass, the minor knolls that covered the plateau were one of the things that gave the grounds their beauty. Several others were the small streams, winding and twisting, moving in many directions here and there, and the many colored wildflowers that stretched from one end of the plateau to the other. There were red-orange poppies and a yellow evening primrose. Rose-crimson lilies and a blue iris. Pink buttercups surrounded by yellow milkweeds. A white madder alongside a blue and white waterleaf, and a row of lavender dayflowers laced with a great many yellow asters.

In the center of the grounds stood Tandara's house. Small by comparison to some of those in the village below, it served its purpose well, not an inch of space unused. With the front door facing north, the outside blended well with the earth surrounding it and the sky above, both in its simple architecture and its color. Panels of burgundy-colored wormwood encircled the entire house. Each panel had been fitted together so well that it was impossible for the naked eye to discern where the openings for the doors and windows were when they were closed. The windows that had been cut on the outside walls to allow sunlight to fill the womb of the house were made of clear but wavy glass, granting Tandara both privacy when needed on certain occasions and a view of her world that was ever-changing as she walked by the paned windows. It was a well-meaning, constant reminder to her of the continuous movement of life itself. But the most magical part of the outside was the minor moat that surrounded the house. Within this furrow was water. Smooth, crystal clear and fluid, with rarely a ripple to charge its spirit. That was indeed part of the game. To see if you could cross to the inside of the house on top of the water without creating a steady but temporary stream of miniature waves.

There were three more characteristic settings on the plateau. The first two were quite noticeable, and contained an unimaginable amount of magic that emanated from within their center. The first was an old well. Its sides were surrounded by a combination of stained and weather-beaten old wood and medium sized stones. Standing several feel high, its strong narrow side beams extended several more feet into the surrounding sky, attaching themselves to a covered pitched roof made of even older worn barked shingles. Extending side to side from each of these side beams was another beam, not square, not quite round in nature, that had as its color an old ragged thick rope made of straw wound around it. Attached to the end of the rope was an aged, faintly colored grayish small bucket. The well itself had no bottom.

The second most detectable element within the landscape was a pyramid-shaped object no larger than a small fist. It was crystal in nature, pure in color, and set on an invisible platform over the stub of an old tree trunk no higher than Cashel herself. The rainbows that emanated from it encircled the entire plateau with its rich flavorful warmth of flushing tints.

The third specific feature that existed on the plateau, unlike the first two, wasn't visible to the naked eye, and was actually made up of three separate but identical elements. They each existed at three different locations on the mountaintop, two toward the front of the house at the edge of the perimeter of the plateau, and one larger one at the rear of the house located in its approximate center, also set on the rim of the plateau. They were large rectangular glass shields, each standing higher than the house itself and extending on either side a greater distance than their height. Had they been apparent when viewed from the sky above, it would have been unmistakably obvious that they formed the three points of a pyramid. Since the time Tandara first made the plateau her home they had remained only pieces of glass, their function denied, their mass nonexistent, not part of the physical world anymore than they were part of any other.

On the inside of the house there were seven rooms, three of which were in the center of the house. They were located within a kind of circular pattern, each room sharing a common interior wall of the other, their exterior wall part of the surrounding circle that led into or out of each room. A small hallway surrounded these three rooms, lighting the way to each from a source unknown to the common eye. In the largest room, that of the only known entry-way into or out of the house, the foundation was covered with a wooden floor. On its own, the floor was beautiful, rich in color in every way and emanating strength and solidity. Not so much to cover its beauty as to maintain it, the wood was covered in certain areas by very large Indian throw rugs, made in one of the villages and given to Tandara as gifts for her friendship. They were radiant, reminders always of just how close she was to those who loved her. And finally, around the perimeter of this room were several floor lamps, starting with the smallest, growing in size as they circled the room, the final lamp coming to within inches of the ceiling.

Several of the other rooms marked to a great degree Tandara's personality. The one she called "The Library" was a medium-sized room, bare except for what appeared to be bookcase wallpaper that surrounded its perimeter, each shelf laced with books of all kinds. The appearance though was deceiving, because in fact from floor to ceiling, top to bottom, stretched across the entire length of the room, sometimes several deep, the books were real physical works of love, each of varying sizes and colors. Their makeup was a distillation of life; philosophy and physics, history and politics, geography and astronomy, mathematics and chemistry and a legion of numerous thoughts and disciplines. In the center of the library were three empty, over-sized upholstered chairs, each facing the nucleus of the room, the round medium-sized coffee table. Transparent and crystal-like, the coffee table was the only sculptured piece of furniture in the room. It was also the most interesting piece of furniture in the entire house. With its base made of the same burgundy wormwood as the outside of the house, the top of the table was inlaid with a type of clear, yet rainbow-colored glass. Like the magic that it was, its illusion always seemed to hold those individuals transfixed who were given the good fortune to be invited to gaze into its depths.

Tandara's bedroom was much like the library in the sense that the only other thing that was obvious as you entered it, outside of the wooden carvings that surrounded her walls, was her bed itself. Much like the path that the old man was traveling on to reach her, her bed was made of crystal clear blue water. Shallow, less than two feet deep, the water had a magic all its own. Hanging over the bed, with its origin at the ceiling was a pyramid-like device that extended its four corners to within several feet of the bed itself, covering and containing the entire garden of water.

The final room was Tandara's kitchen. White was the color of this room, offering the inhabitant the impression of expansiveness. As your eyes moved in an upward motion toward the top of its walls, you quickly realized that there was no noticeable height restraint because there was simply no ceiling covering its space. No blockage for the sun, yet the sunlight entering this area appeared to be filtered, cutting out the harmful rays. Nothing to stop the rain or wind or chill on a cold winter day yet all these weathered components seemed to bounce off an invisible covering of some type when they did appear. For this was the area where Tandara enjoyed her physical sustenance and by her standards and wishes it

would only support those aspects of life that con-
firmed who she was.

Today, in the cool clear breath of fresh air, Tandara
was not to be found in the house. Rather, awaiting
both Cashel and the old man, and the new friend
she was about to make of Dragit, she played on
the grounds. A baby lamb as gentle and beautiful
as you would imagine was enjoying a game of tag
with her. If she would move in one direction the
lamb would move in the other. On occasion,
when she was lucky enough to capture the young
animal, he would sneak between her legs,
nudging her with notification as he moved under
her by shaking his head back and forth, causing
the small golden bell around his neck to send
music through the air.

"Ginruss you are just too smart for me. And on
top of that you can dance around me with a speed
I can only envy. You win again. New to this
reality, you're gaining wisdom at a great speed,
but next time I'll try to out-think your moves."
And with that Tandara sat down on the colorfully
cool green grass. Ginruss, about to jump into her
lap, made a sudden detour and headed for the

The Passage, the Gift, and the Prophecy

edge on one side of the plateau. "Yes, Ginruss, we are going to have a visitor shortly. Actually several. This will be a wonderful and magical day for us all."

The old man was very relaxed lying on his back with his head facing the sky. He almost looked a little funny being fully-clothed and all, with his arms folded over his chest, and a light smile on his lips. But he was indeed in paradise. All the cares of the day were put to rest. Nothing mattered except the moment. That is, of course, until he started bobbing up and down, at times the better portion of his body becoming submerged below the stream.

Coughing and choking he sat up quickly. "Darn it! What's happening? All week strange little things have been occurring to me. I'm losing my control. Think Goble, think. What's going on?"

Slowly, ever so slowly, he again lowered himself onto the stream and allowed his memories to move him back in time to when he had first heard about Tandara. He smiled as he realized that almost ten years to the day had passed. In his mind's eye he reviewed his long friendship and the long barren path he had first climbed to meet Tandara and initiate it. In his memory it had taken days to reach the top of the plateau. Everything seemed to take much longer then. And was usually much harder. Now, his idea of time was enchantingly different. He occupied the majority of his day in a delicious state of nothingness where he mentally floated whenever and wherever he chose. How could anyone not experienced in this illusionary voyage know just how wonderful it really was.

As he floated up the mountain, winding around it in various ways, touching all areas of both his inner and outer world he never came upon either the old path he used to climb or the path Cashel was now on. He stayed only within his own mentally focused playground and drew to him only the energy that he was. At times he would sit up while moving toward the crest of the mountaintop and simply view the beauty around him. He was quite a sight, what with his long grayish white beard and slender figure floating on top of the water rather than in it. But after all, this was a magical journey for him.

Cashel, unaware of all but her immediate focus, had actually passed by Goble's floating body several times now, without either one of them seeing the other. When she had realized the half-way point up the mountain, where she would normally select a wonderfully bright, fresh piece of fruit from one of the trees to garner sustenance and strength from, she was met with disappointment. Reaching out as if to verify what her eyes were telling her, she touched only the remnants of a small, dull prune-like harvest. With her center of thought within, she was emotionally experiencing for the first time a feeling of discord and annoyance with her journey, pangs of irritation seeping into her mental state. Never before had it taken so long to reach Tandara, and never before had the path been so barren. Still straggling somewhat behind her, she momentarily forgot that Dragit was with her this time, and allowed a twinge of unexplored emotion from deep in her soul to surface and find a voice. She seemed to verbalize her thoughts with the wisdom of someone much older, fencing with herself by talking to the air and then answering its questions.

"I don't understand this. There's always been rows of fresh fruit here. I wonder if Tandara knows what's happened . . . probably not. She doesn't come down to the valley much anymore . . . It's been a long time. I wish she would though. Then I wouldn't have to climb this mountain every time I wanted to see her . . . But it's okay I guess. I always have fun and I get to play with Ginruss and Palimar."

Dragit, continuing to walk behind her, raised his head at just the right moment to catch a view of a talkative and animated Cashel. If the wind could talk it would have commented on the small smile beginning to spread across his face. To him, this was Cashel's simple acknowledgment and agreement with many of the comments he had been making during their trek up the mountain. He had wondered many times, in a voice that filled the noncolored air around this huge mound of dirt he called the mountain, why they were making the trip to see Tandara, why she wouldn't come down to see them, why he kept stepping in holes along their path, and why there was nothing to eat along the way, for he was getting awfully hungry.

"Cashel, what was that?"

Now she was back, remembering Dragit trailing right behind her. "What was what?"

"That sound."

"What sound?"

"A man's voice. Something about looking forward to seeing your smiling face."

"Put your hat on, Dragit. You're getting too much sun."

At first he had just mumbled something to himself, then silently and with a disgruntled resignation reached over his shoulder and pulled his hat up over his head.

The Passage, the Gift, and the Prophecy

The lamb was still leaning over the crown of the mountaintop when the old man could be seen ascending the last few feet of its side.

"Goble, my old friend. It's good to see you," shouted Tandara through the gentle wind.

As he pulled himself up from the stream and once again regained his footing, he extended the brightest possible smile in her direction. "And you, Tandara. It's been a long time."

"Much too long."

"I can see Ginruss is still full of the devil," watching him as he darted back and forth between his legs, signaling each pass with the shake of his head and the sound of a bell, as he had done with Tandara. "He's grown a bit. And apparently hasn't forgotten me."

"How could he ever forget you. After all, you were the one that fed him four or five times a day. Look at how fat he's gotten," at which they both laughed. "Tell me, why have you stayed away the length of time you have? I've missed your company. Especially your laughter." The next words were as silent as the fresh fall of snow as they embraced. "Come. Some warm tea and long overdue conversation. We have some catching up to do."

"And your friends. Have they arrived yet?"

Tandara silently smiled through the old man. "You old devil. You're becoming more aware each time I see you. When did you know of my other visitors?"

"When we embraced," was all he answered.

"Cashel seems to have taken a longer path this time to see me. She'll be awhile yet."

"Is that why you sent for me?"

"Goble, I would never send for you . . . although I might gently suggest a visit. But your insight's not too far off. Cashel's development is only now beginning to stretch. In a way she's approaching a fork in the road. And it seems that her perception is leading her in the same direction most physicals eventually choose. Some of the wonder she normally sees is being pushed aside for those thoughts that keep one focused on only physical reality. I thought if she had the chance to meet you, that you and I together might be able to help nudge her in the right direction a little sooner."

"And her friend."

"Not her friend actually, but one of her brother's. He's about to begin his journey. I thought together we might be able to help him also. But either way, we still have a lot of time to ourselves before they arrive. There's much to talk about." And with that they both entered the house that was Tandara's.

The sky outside remained the color of a beautiful light blue with golden white clouds for as far as the eye could see. Not a dark one in the bunch. Except for the path that Cashel and Dragit were on. Here the trail was now wet, a multicolored sprinkle falling from high above. Normally Cashel would have enjoyed a light afternoon shower, but today was anything but normal for her, especially with Dragit's irritation at getting wet.

Dragit looked up at the sky and just shook his head. "Why do you think the rest of the mountain isn't getting wet? It's only where we're walking. Isn't there another path we can take? Maybe there's one somewhere that leads down the mountain."

"You're not the only one getting drenched. But complaining about it isn't going to help either one of us. Can't you think about how beautiful the rain is?"

"This must be some of the magic you were telling me about. The rest of the mountain's dry and we're getting rained on."

Cashel had stopped listening to him. She had her own troubles. The holes on the dirt-lined passage were beginning to fill with water and every now and then she would inadvertently step into one, her shoes and socks becoming soggy and making her squish as she walked. But, being the positive person she was, she thought that if she began to sing she might be able to take her mind off these minor obstacles that seemed to be befalling her. It didn't help. Her singing was constantly interrupted by Dragit's comments every time he also stepped into a hole. Cashel was still getting wet and her normally pleasant mood was starting to waver. But she didn't stop. Trying to override her brother's pronouncements she continued her walk, trying her best to outmaneuver the blemished ground and its containment of pools of water. With invented lyrics that told stories of Ginruss and Palimar, her voice became strong and sure, building in volume to drown out Dragit's.

Focused as she was on both her singing and her drive to the mountaintop, Cashel didn't seem to notice the pleasant warm wind that engulfed her each time she mentioned Palimar. Unknown and hidden, Palimar was with her, her gentle, loving horse, softly nudging from behind, helping to carry her along the pass and through the light rain. There was, however, a strong sense within her of the wind at her back, and at times its harshness in moving her forward. For in her mind she needed to maintain her thoughts of what awaited her at the mountaintop if she was to survive the climb.

The Passage, the Gift, and the Prophecy

In the distance she could just see the entrance to the tunnel that would carry them on the final leg of their journey to the plateau. And for the first time in awhile she started to smile, knowing that the tunnel would shelter them from the wet sky. But as they approached and entered she noticed that while the initial portion of the tunnel appeared to be bathed in light, further on, beyond her view, the color of darkness would overtake her if she continued to walk. This frightened her enough to stop and momentarily wonder if she was really on the right path, for never before had she noticed a lack of light within the tunnel. This whole day was becoming quite a new experience for her. Just as it was for Dragit, who for the first time since beginning this journey with her, had sensed her uneasiness and loss of knowing and knew he had to keep his comments to himself and allow her to think.

Just a tab self-absorbed and a mite frightened, she struggled on through this new world of darkness the tunnel had offered her. Holding Dragit's hand in one of her own, she began feeling her way as she moved through it, pressing her free hand on the sides of its unfamiliar walls, sensing their full rich texture. She intuitively began picking up images of those who had previously walked this path before her, and in so doing, once again began feeling lighthearted. And as her essence regained its peacefulness, she began to feel stronger and more spirited. What she hadn't noticed, nor was she able to piece together in her mind, was that not hearing a word from Dragit since they had entered the tunnel, had actually began to change her mood. The heaviness had began to lift, returning the familiar light of harmony to her. Several more minutes and she was once again back in the open viewing the beautiful sky before her. Magically, the shower that had descended on them when they had entered the tunnel had disappeared.

In a very short time they had reached the crest of the ridge that put them in sight of the plateau that was home to Tandara. "Hello. Is anyone there?" came the tiny voice that was Cashel's. "Can anyone hear me?" She thought she heard a response but couldn't be sure, for whatever vocals had been transmitted to her had been caught up in the wind and dispersed. "Hello! Is anyone there? It's Cashel." This time she heard it. Loud and vibrant there was no mistaking Ginruss' welcome. The warm and wonderful music of a baby lamb's voice, mixing with the sound of a small golden bell, filled the afternoon air with the sweetest melody Cashel had heard all day.

Chapter Two

As they crossed the last few hundred feet to the plateau, Cashel and Dragit finally came within view of Ginruss, who by this time was bobbing his neck up and down and then darting back and forth waiting for her. "Bah, bah, bah," was his heightened call.

"I'm coming Ginruss, I'm coming." Hearing Ginruss' voice float through the air, Cashel momentarily forgot her brother, excitedly racing to her four-legged friend. She now planted both feet solidly on the grass-lined plateau and became as passionate as Ginruss, holding onto him, moving her hands over his coat, rubbing him this way and that. "Oh Ginruss, I've missed you too. I wish you were able to come and see me so it wouldn't be so long between visits."

Dragit on the other hand made the decision not to join in his sister's enthusiasm, selecting instead to keep his own company, his own state of mind. As he searched the plateau, his eyes located and then focused on what appeared to be a mound of soft green grass, a number of yards from where Cashel and Ginruss were having their reunion. Starting for it, Dragit was momentarily unaware that with each step he sank further and further into the path he was moving over. When he reached the mound he began to lower himself only to find the ground was coming up to meet him rather quickly. Already knee-deep into the knoll, he touched the ground easily with his hands as he began to bend his body ever so slightly forward. Realizing what had happened, he could feel his own concern growing, his heart racing a little faster than usual. His call was gentle at first, although with each succeeding call of her name, the cascade of his voice gave the anxious feeling within him away. "Cashel! . . . Cashel!"

Absorbed in both their conversation and each other's company, neither Tandara nor Goble heard the commotion outside the house. That is until Ginruss made a focused run at Dragit, jumping around him, stopping once or twice to lick his face, which was now almost eye level to him, and then making another committed charge toward one of the front windows, lifting himself on his two hind legs, sticking his head into the window and excitedly trying to tell his two friends that they had some visitors.

"Will you look at that old lamb of mine," was all Tandara could say.

"Old lamb?"

"Okay then. Young lamb aged beyond his years."

"Do you think Ginruss is trying to tell us something?"

"I believe he's either eaten some loco weed or Cashel and her brother have just arrived."

"I'll vote for your friend Cashel and her brother. After what you've told me so far I look forward to meeting them."

All three of them, Tandara, Goble, and Cashel, each from their side of the wall of the house that separated them, headed for the window Ginruss was attached to, reaching him after he had made a halfhearted attempt to jump into the house. He had missed his mark, his body now straddling the windowsill, half in and half out. Cashel, with more immediate concern for what trouble Ginruss had gotten himself into than her brother's ever-growing vocal protests, made a feeble attempt to help him. Thinking of him first and not watching her footing as she moved toward him, she made a blunder of her own, stepping instantly into a freshly troweled hole Ginruss had made earlier in the day. From that misstep her other foot followed suit and planted itself directly into the narrow moat that surrounded the house, the one Ginruss had just traversed without raising a ripple. Trying to correct her movements she bungled again and inadvertently lunged backwards, within seconds finding herself sprawled half in and half out of the moat, her face covered with dirt and grass cuttings and the rest of her body now wet. Taking a momentary second to laugh at herself, she then reached up and tickled Ginruss' underbelly causing him to squirm and bleat until he had worked himself into the house over the protests of Tandara and Goble.

What Cashel wasn't able to immediately see was that as Ginruss left the windowsill he landed on Tandara's stomach rather than the floor, his small body pinning her to the ground. Collecting herself, Cashel managed to grab hold of the ledge and look in through the window after him.

Goble was in good spirits, laughing at Tandara's situation and her unfamiliar loss of control of Ginruss.

"Alright, you small uncut blanket, you. You've made it into the house, but I'm not part of the flooring. Off," was all she said before Ginruss started licking her face.

Cashel, thinking she had caused the predicament, tried to reach Ginruss from behind to move him, only to extend too far in through the window herself, following Ginruss' lead and falling on top of the only part of Tandara that Ginruss wasn't occupying. An invisible moment seemed to pass before Cashel found herself and Ginruss both being lifted into the air by unfamiliar arms.

Looking up, Cashel noticed the most wonderful smile she had ever seen, followed by a beautiful melodic voice as both Ginruss and herself were being gently lowered to a spot beside Tandara's reclining body.

"I've enjoyed this immensely, but I can't laugh anymore without it hurting."

Picking herself up, Tandara just stared at Ginruss and Cashel and began shaking her head. "If I'd of known I was going to become a mattress for the two of you, I would have eaten more over the summer to fatten myself up."

A sheepish smile followed by the words "I feel silly," was about all Cashel could say.

Staring up at both Tandara and Goble, Cashel's sheepish smile expanded, lighting the room. Goble's smile then began again, followed by Tandara, answering with one of her own.

"I've missed you so much," was all Cashel could get out before falling into a now standing Tandara's open arms.

"I've missed you too, you little enchantress. I want to introduce a very good friend of mine to you. Someone you've heard me talk about from time to time."

"Goble!"

Tandara smiled. "That's very good. Quite perceptive."

"You know me?"

Tandara was pleased. "I think your beard gave you away. If I remember, I described you in detail."

All Cashel could do was smile and shake her head from side to side. "Not the beard."

"His height?"

A continued smile also discounting his height was the only response from Cashel. "I sensed Goble would be here just before we crested the plateau."

Tandara to Goble. "Do you see what I mean. She has the magic within her."

"I feel as though I want to give you a hug Cashel, hope you don't mind," whereupon Goble did just that.

"You know my name also," she smiled, returning the hug.

Goble didn't have a chance to respond. From outside, on the wings of a gentle breeze, Dragit's voice was becoming one of alarm. "Cashel!! . . . Cashel!!"

"You're brother?

"Oh, I forgot. He was sinking into the ground. I think he's having a bit of a problem."

"Cashel, did you tell your brother what you had experienced your first time up here or did you forget?"

Another sheepish grin.

"Cashel!!! . . . Cashel!!!"

Putting aside their conversation and moving toward the door to the outside, Tandara, Goble and Cashel, followed by a frisky young lamb, made their way toward Dragit's elevating calls.

With his last call to Cashel, Dragit began sinking deeper, only his upper torso now visible to his charging rescuers. The lower he went the wilder his screams, and the wilder his screams, the more energy he used and the lower he went. Coupled with his flailing arms he was quite a sight to look at.

"We're coming Dragit, we're coming. We'll be there in just a min . . ." Slip. Now Cashel was on the ground.

"I've got her. You go on to her brother."

Tandara was on him. Smiling her little smile which was louder than any action he was making, even his bellowing calls for his sister. "Dragit. Stop doing what you're doing for a second. Listen to me. There's only one way to get you out of there, and it isn't pulling you out. Only you can do it."

"Why can't you just take my hand?"

"All I would be able to do is to hold it. I don't have the strength to pull you out."

By this time both Goble and Cashel had joined the two. Cashel, even with Dragit's immediate problem, was unable to contain her laughter at her brother's plight.

Goble on the other hand, was only smiling down at him.

"What about you? You're big enough to pull me out of this."

"Only you can pull yourself out. I'll assist you if you like, but it's up to you."

"Why won't you help me?"

"I will help you. I'll help you to help yourself. But first you've got to relax."

"Are you out of your mind. How can I relax when I can't move to help myself and the ground keeps swallowing me up? It's like a big mouth that won't stop chewing."

"Dragit, will you listen to them? They're trying to help you."

"Cashel will you please get me out of here!!!!"

"Close your eyes for a minute Dragit."

"You're crazy. If I close my eyes you might be the last thing I see. That's not very funny."

As Tandara turned and glanced at Ginruss, he knew it was his turn to try. And try he did, first by running circles around Dragit and then by stopping every so often to lick his face. It was working. Dragit's focus on his captured body was changing to complete wonder as he noticed that no one was moving to help him and some crazy small lamb was running a ring around him. Confusion set in and he didn't know whether to laugh or cry. His mind stopped working. It seemed nothing was his choice anymore. He did notice, however, that each time Ginruss bent to kiss him he inadvertently closed his eyes, thinking of course that he could avoid the lamb's sloppy licks. Tandara saw her chance and took it. "Dragit, Ginruss will stop licking you if you think of him licking Cashel instead."

"What!?"

"Just see him in your mind licking Cashel and he'll stop."

Dragit was alone in his hole. He tried Tandara's vision and was very surprised. Ginruss had moved over to Cashel and was kissing her all over.

His quizzical glance was Goble's opening. "Dragit! Close your eyes just as you did when Ginruss started licking you and see yourself on top of the ground. That's all you need to do to get out of your hole."

"You people are all crazy. Cashel, will you please stop playing with that lamb and help me out of here!?"

But she wasn't listening. Ginruss and her were involved in a gentle battle to see who could tease the other the most. He was winning. Her face glistened from all his affection.

He was going deeper and you could see and feel the fear surround him. With an upward glance, first at Tandara and then over at Goble, he made a decision. He closed his eyes and concentrated. And within a magical second, although still covered with flecks of dirt and grass, he was on top of the ground. As was his nature, the fear receded into a nervous laugh. "I don't understand. How? Why? What did I . . .?"

"See, we're not really crazy. It worked!" And with that Tandara turned with Goble and walked back to the house.

Now within feet of the front door, Goble momentarily returned his gaze to Dragit, missed where he was walking and tripped over his own feet, falling head first into the moat. Tandara held her hand to her mouth trying hard not to laugh, but Dragit wasn't so polite. Cashel on the other hand, was still so involved with Ginruss that she failed to notice either Dragit's release from the ground or Goble's folly. That is until she overheard her brother's laughter and followed his pointed finger toward the moat and a very wet Goble.

"That's the second time today I've become more attached to the water than I really wanted to. I feel like I'm losing control."

Tandara gave Goble a stern but helpful look. "You know better than to think you ever had control. Dominion, my dear friend, not domination. Allow your energy to flow into and become a part of the energy that surrounds you. Don't expect the encircling nourishment to conform to you."

"You're right. Thank you for the reminder . . . Three students, one teacher."

Tandara smiled that elusive all-knowing smile. "Almost . . . I rather enjoy thinking of it as four students, four teachers. And just about now a lesson is about to be given. Look over at our friends.

Standing next to Cashel, Dragit was brushing the earth off his clothes. "Well, I can tell you were really concerned. You didn't even bother to help."

"Oh, but I did help."

"How? All you did was play with that piece of wool."

That did it. Now Cashel was becoming a little annoyed with Dragit. "This piece of wool helped you also. Without him you wouldn't have been able to focus enough on what was necessary to pull yourself out of your predicament. He helped you take your mind off yourself and what you didn't like, and focus on what you wanted instead." And now it was Cashel's turn to rotate her body and move away from Dragit, step by step, one foot in front of the other, moving her back toward the house to visit her friends. Behind her a small happy lamb was in tow.

After having just been admonished by his sister, he did the only thing he could to save face. He walked back over to the same spot he had just come up from, sat down over it as if to show the ground beneath him who was boss, and looked toward the sky as though contemplating the greater questions of the universe.

When Cashel reached the front of the house, her inner sense was a combination of amusement and irritation. A strange combination for her indeed. Her internal enchantment was usually with her. But the irritation. That was new. Especially toward her brother. And it bothered her. When she reached the front door she turned and bent down to meet Ginruss' eyes, telling him she was going in, but he needed to remain outside. Acknowledging her firmness and still full of unused energy, he began circling the house at a comfortable gait.

She spotted Tandara and Goble almost immediately. "I'm sorry about all that. Part my fault, I guess. I'll have to have a talk with him when he calms down a little bit."

"Don't you mean when you calm down a little bit?"

"I don't know what's making me so irritated with him."

A quick change of subject was part of Tandara's magical way of communicating when she wanted you to come to some kind of conclusion yourself. She usually started as she did this time, by interjecting a smile and a comment. "Before we had to run outside I wanted to tell you that Goble and I were talking about how far you've come over the last year in your learning."

"I'm proud of myself. And very thankful I have you as a teacher. You're so patient with me."

"You're wrong, Cashel. I'm not patient with you. To have patience is to believe that something will take a certain amount of time for it to happen. I don't believe any such thing."

"I don't understand."

"Everything has its place. Its time. Now or then, it doesn't matter. It all exists now in our minds. So at anytime we chose we can make something happen. Patience isn't necessary. Just like Dragit digging himself out from the hole he found himself in. When we're ready we can have the thought and create anything we want. Again I say to you, patience isn't necessary."

Seeing her student deep in thought was when the lessons really began. "Now I feel like teasing you a little. Did you know that when Goble decided to visit he started from the bottom of the mountain long after you did and arrived quite a bit before you?"

Cashel turned to Goble with a quizzical look. "I started out just when the sun was beginning to show itself."

"And I began my journey around noontime, beginning as Tandara had said, from the base of the mountain."

The look on Cashel's face said it all. She was stunned. "I don't understand. I didn't see you pass me."

Tandara immediately took the lead. "Why don't we all sit down? Cashel, you must be very tired. You've been walking a long time to get here, and Ginruss could wear out a saint."

"I don't understand, Goble. How did you get here before me, if you left after me? It's just not possible."

"All things are possible on my mountain, Cashel. You of all people should know that."

Goble's comment was a little more stern. "There are many paths that lead to Tandara. Not just the one you were on."

"But I've never seen another path up the mountain before."

Tandara was at first silent, exchanging knowing glances with Goble before speaking. "When you're ready to see another path, it'll be there for you. Much in the same way Palimar was there for you when you were ready to see him."

"I still don't understand."

While Goble and Cashel continued to talk, Tandara excused herself and left the room. Once reaching her library she searched the walls until her eyes landed on what she wanted. With the slight twist of her wrist, what appeared to be a small bundle of old papers several feet higher than herself removed themselves from one of the shelves and floated downward into her waiting hands. Somewhat less than an inch thick, the papers resembled an oversized unbound book, ancient in sight and feeling, the writing laid delicately on sheets of old papyrus.

Much like old photographs not having been looked at for years, Tandara spent some time retracing her own thoughts as she moved through the manuscript, page by delicate page. Returning almost an hour later she handed the manuscript to Cashel. "As promised." Laced in gold with white lettering the manuscript was held together by a blue and white braided yarn, tied at the center of the cover page which boldly stated, *Gifts of Perception.*

Both Goble and Tandara watched as Cashel's smile lit the room on fire. "This is the gift you promised me."

"Yes. And I guarantee you won't be disappointed.

"Cashel and I had a wonderful visit. You were gone just long enough to give us each a chance to get to know the other. As always, you're timing was perfect."

Cashel was confused. "I don't understand. You just left a minute ago. Yet, Goble and I talked for a long time."

"I think you were engaged with Goble's stories so deeply that time just sort of stood still for you. How wonderful. That's experiencing life the way it was meant to be."

"What do you mean the way it was meant to be?"

"Caught in the gulf between time and space. Not remembering the past. Not projecting into the future. Thought standing still. Focused only on what you're involved in at the moment."

"Is that possible?"

Goble took the lead on this one. "Not only possible but guaranteed. Whenever we're so focused on something, a person or event say, well, we're caught in our own little world and the time around us just keeps moving."

"Caught in our own world?"

"Cashel, look at the title of the manuscript I just handed you."

"*Gifts of Perception*. What does it mean?"

"That we each see what we want to. And sometimes that includes our idea of time and how we move about in it. But you have to read it for yourself to get the greatest benefit from its message. It wouldn't help you if I tried to explain all of it to you. You would only hear what you chose to. It's much better for you to read its wisdom yourself and allow your own ideas to bring its meaning to life."

"If it helps, Cashel, Tandara once gave me a copy of the very same manuscript. It's a wonderful guide for all of us. It helped open me up quite a bit. Allowed me to see worlds I had yet to explore. My guess is it'll do the same for you. But you read it and see how you feel."

Caught in their own moments, none of the three noticed a small figure enter the door, take a step in and slip on the throw rug below him. That is until Dragit shot through the air and landed with a thud into an invisible glass wall before him. "Ahhhhhh!

"Dragit!"

"I'm not sure I like this place."

"Dragit, come sit down with us. Cashel has something to tell you and we really haven't been introduced yet."

Dragit, slightly bent and holding his back with one hand and his nose with the other, made his way to the three.

"Is anything else going to happen to me while I'm here? This is a strange place."

With a smile made of sheer warmth, Tandara put her arm around Dragit and he melted.

"You're a pretty interesting customer yourself. My friend who looks like your grandfather is Goble and . . .

"How did you know he looks like my grand-father?"

"I saw you image him."

"What?"

Goble now took Dragit by the hand and in much the way of a philosophic grandfather, sat him down beside him. "Remember how you imagined yourself out of the hole?"

"Yeah."

"That's how Tandara was able to see your grandfather. She looked at the images running around in your head."

"No one can do that."

"Tandara can do that. All of the time if she chooses. I can do that some of the time and your sister is beginning to learn how to do it also. And after a while, if you want it, we'll teach you how to do it."

"This is a magical place, Dragit. Like I told you before we came here. You didn't believe me then. But you've already experienced some of the magic."

"Getting stuck in the ground isn't magic."

"Are you sure? When was the last time you got stuck in the ground? . . . You see? It is magic if it's what got you stuck to begin with and then got you unstuck later."

"I got me unstuck. You guys wouldn't help."

"They all smiled that little knowing smile. Now Tandara took Dragit's hand. "In a way you're right. You got you unstuck. Not us. All we did was to remind you of just how powerful you are. How powerful your thoughts are. It's your thoughts that are the magic, Dragit. Your thoughts. And you formed them. To get you into the hole in the first place and then to get you out."

"I think you guys are goofy. I didn't want to get myself stuck in the ground." And with what seemed like the last bit of oxygen in the room, Dragit tried to tell them he didn't do that to himself. But he didn't quite make it. His mouth was now opening and closing at a much slower speed, releasing fewer and fewer words, his eyes already starting to close. Without formality of any kind, his body began showing signs that it was looking for that transitional rest where it tries to incorporate the changing weight of the air from the valley below.

"The thinness of the air up here is helping to relax him. How about you Cashel, how do you feel? Is that a yawn I just saw? I thought so. How would you both like to take a bit of a nap?" Cashel was first to try and answer as Tandara turned to her and stroked her hair. "You had a much longer journey up here than you had last time. I forgot just how tired you might be when you arrived. Why don't you take my bed, and Dragit can sleep for a while in the meditation room."

"I thought we'd never get here. It was a much harder climb this time."

"We can discuss that later, after you wake up from your nap. Follow me my lady, and I'll introduce you to a magical cradle." Goble, if you can hold our friend up here for a moment, I'll be right back to lead him to his resting spot." And with that Tandara took a yawning Cashel by the hand and led her down the hallway towards her bedroom.

Almost out of earshot and barely able to keep her eyes open she heard Goble's melodious voice call after her. "Try to read a page or so of the manuscript before you fall asleep and then try putting it under your pillow before you close your eyes. It'll help you retain its secrets."

Several moments passed before Tandara reappeared to take Dragit into the meditation room where a second bed awaited him. He looked semi-conscious and willing to follow anyone anywhere. Down the hall to one of the three rooms at the center of the house was their destination.

Satisfied that he had passed on some good advice to Cashel and had kept Dragit somewhat awake until Tandara returned for him, Goble strolled toward the front door, opened it and stepped outside.

He was a little surprised. The air was not as fresh as he remembered from several hours ago. There was a misty smell all around, carried through the lowering sky by little puffs of wind. No matter which way he turned he wasn't able to see the edge of the plateau in any direction without complete concentration and focus on its ending point. And even then it was somewhat hazy. What he was able to notice was the distinct outline of both Ginruss and Palimar who seemed to be standing next to and gazing into the pyramid-shaped crystal that was lazily suspended on its invisible platform, several inches over the old tree stump.

Making his way through the small drafts of wind that were much stronger than Goble had suspected, he found his destination alongside his two furry friends and much like them, aligned his gaze with theirs, deep within the fist-sized crystal. What he saw was both surprising and fascinating, even so in recognition. For long ago, Tandara had told him the story about the Hollows

The Passage, the Gift, and the Prophecy

and that one day they may try to return. Their time had apparently come.

Much like the glass-laden crystal that covered the coffee table, this crystal also projected for its viewers a glimpse into the immediate future. Within its depths was a glimpse of the scenario of what was to follow the cloudy vapor that had begun to cover the top of the plateau. With his strength of convictions Goble broke the vision's hold on his senses and began walking back toward the house. As he approached, Tandara was standing in the doorway, arms outstretched, an invitation to a hug. "I know," were the only words she passed to Goble as he accepted her offer.

"Since you first told me about the Hollows I've always wanted to know more. I find this very interesting but Cashel and Dragit sure picked an odd time for a visit."

"You now know as well as I that there are no accidents. Their being here today may well have been an unconscious decision on their part, but on some level they made the choice to come."

"Are they asleep?"

"More or less. I guess you could say that Cashel's very relaxed but awake. She's drawing energy from the pyramid over the bed and at last glance was taking your advice, reading a little bit before closing her eyes. She even asked if the manuscript would get wet if she laid it under the pillow before she fell asleep."

"This must be quite an experience for her, laying on a bed made of water with a funny gizmo suspended above her. My guess is that she'll have a lot of questions for you when she gets up."

"She's within the energy of the house. Her questions will become secondary to her experience. And of course she is a very willing student. She has an open heart and trusts both of us, knowing that love will be her only guide."

"As for Dragit. He was asleep the moment his body hit the bed. The rest will be good for him. It'll make his experience much more valuable as we go through this."

"Tandara, have you ever mentioned the Hollows to Cashel?"

"There was never a need. Her growth is not yet where yours was when we first discussed them. Why don't you and I take a look and see where they are now. It should help us plan our time better." As Goble nodded his head in agreement, both he and Tandara made their way to the coffee table that marked the center of the room within the library.

Now seated on the large, overstuffed chairs, both Tandara and Goble were focused on the overlaid glass crystal tabletop and its translucent depths. The Hollows were both apparent and visible, entering the mountain at its base and beginning their climb toward the top. For several hours while Cashel and Dragit slept, the two friends watched the ascent of the Hollows, most of the time in silence. The sound of the wind continued its howling, at times reaching an incredibly high-pitched fevered rhapsody of an unwelcome proportion. Tandara was about to break their silence and share some thoughts with Goble when out of the corner of her eye she noticed a creature at the entrance to this room of books, this room of archives.

Chapter Three

Cashel, holding the manuscript next to her heart, appeared before them clothed in Tandara's colorful bathrobe and was all smiles. It didn't seem to matter that the robe reached to the floor and beyond. "Is it okay? This is so beautiful."

Surprised and amused, both Tandara and Goble couldn't help but laugh. Tandara was the first to recover. "You may have it if you like, but I think we may have to shorten it a bit."

"Oh thank you, Tandara. What are you both doing?"

"How was your nap?"

"I feel like I've slept forever."

"The bed has a way of doing that."

"That's the most wonderful bed I've ever slept in. What's that thing hanging over it?"

"The Pyramid. When you're under it, it helps your body to rest and heal, and allows your mind to reach a greater state of awareness or higher consciousness. And the water that was your mattress, helps to balance the charge your body is getting from the pyramid. All in all, the different energies of the pyramid work together to realign you spiritually. You should feel much more energetic and alive after just a few minutes in the bed, although it'll seem as though you've slept a long time."

"How come I didn't fall into the water? I was laying on top of it."

After Goble's recent experience with the stream up the mountain he hesitated a moment, then spoke. "Cashel, one of these days you'll do that naturally, knowing it's possible. But right now your awake self still doesn't completely believe it's possible. So Tandara and the energy within the house helped make you very tired so you'd forget that it wasn't possible to lay on the water without sinking."

"I get it. You tricked me to make me see something in a different way. Kind of like a gift."

"Yes. A gift of perception."

"The manuscript!"

"Yes, the manuscript."

"Cashel, come join us. Tandara has something to show you."

That was a surprise. And Tandara stared long and hard at Goble. "I'm not so sure."

"You said she was growing and changing. And that the choice to be here was hers. What better time to introduce her to . . ."

The wail from the wind was loud and piercing, threatening the quiet of the remaining day. From outside we could hear Ginruss' concern, while inside Cashel made her way quickly to Tandara's side. Softly at first, growing louder with each passing moment, they heard the sound of a light sprinkle hitting the roof and the sides of the house. They all knew that a flood of water was about to fall from an ever darkening sky.

Forgetting her initial fear of the bellowing and beginning gale she began to think of Ginruss. "Ginruss is going to get wet. And I thought I heard Palimar out there with him. Can I go and get them and bring them in?"

"Ginruss will find his own shelter as he always has and Palimar needs none. You forget that Palimar isn't physical as Ginruss and the three of us. They'll be fine. Besides. For the moment we have bigger fish to fry."

Glancing down at the coffee table and through its superficial skin, Tandara motioned for Cashel to take her fill of what lay before her. What was immediately apparent was a three-dimensional picture or holograph of the mountain they were on, the mountain she had climbed just a short time ago to visit Tandara. There also appeared to be a dark mist, a fog at this point, not yet clearly defined, winding its way around the base while continuing to move in a spiraling upward direction. Encompassing everything it touched, it moved with precision over the landscape, changing the light color of the brownish sandstone clay that was the mountain's outer skin, and the lush green brush that grew along and over its exterior, into a far darker aspect of itself. Moving, turning and twisting, it was slowly making its way toward the crest of the plateau.

After a moment or two of viewing what was before her, Cashel, unconsciously and somewhat imperceptibly, began backing away from the coffee table. "What is that horrible stuff."

"The Hollows."

"The what?"

"The Hollows. Unfortunately they aren't very friendly, and they're coming in our direction."

Goble had momentarily moved to the side of the room to retrieve something from a small white box. He had watched Tandara place the box on one of the lower shelves the last time he had visited with her and instinctively knew that its contents were to be used over the next several days. Bending to retrieve it, he reached over and gently removed it from its position on the shelf. He then gingerly began to remove its cover and expose its contents of seven white candles. Each candle was extremely thin, and even though quite long in nature, gave one the impression that its working duration would be very short. As Goble picked one up to examine it, he noticed that its wick had a whitish blue tint to it and stretched not only the length of its measure, but continued on winding its way around itself from top to bottom.

Walking back to his friends, Goble's brow furrowed, exposing a somewhat quizzical look under his normally expressionless face. Noticing his uneasiness Tandara took the lead. "One for each room of the house. Each candle will draw its energy from its individual point of identity within each room. The exception to that would be the three rooms at the center that surround and touch each other. For each of those rooms, a candle should be placed in front of the doorway guarding its entrance."

Glancing from Tandara to the coffee table to Goble, Cashel's soft voice formed a potent declaration and in doing so made herself known. "If you'll let me, I'd like to help."

"Good! This is now a part of your reality, too, Cashel. It'll take all four of us working together to accomplish what we need to."

"All four of us? I don't think Dragit's going to help much. He's pretty irritated at me for bringing him."

"Well, you know your brother better than I do, but my guess is that he'll come around. But before we fulfill our task with the candles, there's still enough time to introduce you to the Hollows and talk a little bit about the manuscript."

"Can we talk about the Hollows first?"

Tandara's head tilted ever so slightly to one side and once again she smiled at her small friend. "The Hollows first, but just to tell you who they are. Your concentration needs to be on the manuscript right now."

As Goble motioned silently to Tandara, he received an almost imperceptible response. A simple slight nod of her head granting him the right of explanation. Now he only needed to come up with a way to illustrate and describe to her who the Hollows were. Start simply he thought. After a moment's contemplation he had it. "They're spirits, Cashel, spirits. Rather unique spirits actually. The name given to them a long time ago, the Hollows, describes that uniqueness very well."

"Palimar's unique. There's no one like him anywhere."

"You're right. Palimar is unique. And very special. But it's not really the same. Palimar can come and go between dimensions. When he's in his own dimension he's wrapped in a visual expansion of pure energy. When he enters our dimension he's bound by agreement to take on a physical body. Those are the rules of our physical reality. To remain you must be a part of it in all ways."

"But he's neither total energy or physical."

"You're right. Here on the mountain, because of an agreement he has with Tandara, he's allowed to utilize both to create a third visual. So when we see him, his energy outlines his physical body. He's immersed in his energy. Totally and completely. Nothing can influence or harm him but his own thoughts. And in the state he's in, he's learned to solidly focus and maintain a running stream of positive thoughts all the time. The Hollows uniqueness is a little different."

Tandara had become very silent during their exchange on the Hollows. She wanted Cashel to know more about them, yet, because of them, felt that she needed to move Cashel's attention toward the manuscript. "Maybe we could change directions for a moment?"

Goble knew immediately. "Yes, that's a good idea. Cashel, how much of Tandara's manuscript did you read before falling asleep?"

"I tried to read a lot. But every time I'd read something my eyes would start closing. They started feeling real heavy. And then I'd start getting lightheaded. And then I'd read some more and my eyes would start closing again. That's never happened to me before. It made me real tired. But when I woke up, I opened it and looked through it, and everything I read seemed like I already knew it."

Tandara passed on a motherly expression when she replied, "Reading and remembering is what made you real tired and a little light-headed."

"Remembering what?"

Now Tandara's smile was wide. "Things you already know."

Moving her head back and forth between her two teachers, Cashel's eyes were now on Goble who responded to her questions. "Do you remember reading anything that said that your belief about something will only allow you to perceive it in one way. That whatever stream of thoughts you have about a particular thing, won't allow you to see anything else about it until you're open to it?"

"Yes. What exactly does that mean?"

"That you get what you believe. If you think that the only color for the sky is blue and the only color for the grass is green, then that's all you'll see, no matter what the color really is."

"What about having a belief that I could be just like Tandara."

Goble was thoughtful, trying to provide Cashel with the right answer. "Yes and no. Yes, because whatever you really believe, whatever you hold within your heart, will become yours. And, depending on just how much you believe it, how much energy and emotion you put behind your belief, will determine just how quickly you get it. But also no. No, because each one of us is an individual. Unique to ourselves and each other. No one could ever be exactly like another person."

"Let me see if I can help," said a thoughtful Tandara. "Do you remember earlier today when you were climbing the mountain to come to see me?"

"Of course."

"Do you remember commenting on the lack of fresh fruit to be found and then wondering if I knew what had happened to the fruit that had always been there? And then thinking that I didn't know about it because I didn't go down to the valley much anymore?"

"You heard me? We were only halfway up the mountain. How is that possible?"

"You forget. I can read the energy around you. Right now. Your comments and feelings are still with you. All that's happening this moment and all that's happened before. And a portion of where you're projecting your energy into the future. Now, am I right?"

Silence. With eyes as big as small plums, Cashel was amazed to hear her private conversation expressed by Tandara, who was now looking at her stunned expression while grinning from ear to ear.

Slowly and quietly Cashel answered Tandara's query and formed the word "Yes."

"And do you remember saying that if I came down to the valley more often you wouldn't have to climb the mountain every time you wanted to see me?"

First her eyes grew from small plums to large oranges and then she dropped her head before answering with another barely audible "yes."

Goble reached out and put his arm around Cashel, pulling her close to his side. "What you really believe. What you hold within your heart, will become yours."

"I don't understand."

Tandara now looked deeply into Cashel's eyes and asked, "Have you been arguing with your brothers and sisters since the last time I saw you?"

"Yes. Especially Dragit."

"About what?"

Once again, Cashel chose to drop her head before lightly expressing herself. "You."

An all-knowing Tandara was still smiling. "It's okay, Cashel. That was bound to happen sooner or later. It's really okay."

"They think you're a little strange living way up here rather than in the valley with the rest of us."

"Strange means different, and I am indeed different. Remember what Goble just said. That each of us is unique. That no two of us are alike."

"Yes."

"All of the people from the valley that visit me are different from each other. And many of them come to visit because they like the differences my personality and lifestyle suggest to them. That includes your brothers and sisters. But right now they're a little jealous of the close relationship you and I have with each other. In time that'll change."

"I think that Dragit's jealous of our friendship."

Goble was bending to meet Cashel's eyes. "Cashel, listen to me. Dragit is a good person. All good people have within them human emotions. Some good, some not so good. Some strong, some weak. But one thing's for sure. These same emotions are shared by all of us. It's simply how we choose to use them at any given moment. Your brothers' and sisters' thoughts about Tandara and the mountain over the last week or so have influenced your moods. They did something very human. And you responded in kind. They planted little thoughts of unrest within you. Those thoughts centered on Tandara and the mountain. They didn't do it to hurt you. It wasn't intentional. They were reacting out of jealousy. Do you understand?"

"I think so."

"Very simply, the seeds that they planted stayed with you. It was that kind of uneasiness within you that colored your perception as you climbed the path today to see Tandara."

"I think I'm beginning to understand. You're telling me that I allowed their comments about Tandara and the mountain to color my feelings

. . . about how much I enjoyed coming up here. And that if I hadn't of listened to them . . ."

"No, no, no. Listen to everyone. Just allow each person their own perception if it's different than yours, without allowing their opinions to effect your feelings about the same thing."

"You mean that if my feelings had been strong enough about my own beliefs then their comments would have never influenced me?"

"Yes."

"And that I would have had an easier time climbing the path with Dragit?"

"Yes. Absolutely. Never assume someone else's comments about anything or anyone are more of a truth than your own feelings. Your view is the only one that really counts. Your brothers and sisters are important. Dragit is important. But your own inner knowing about what you feel, what you believe, has to prevail."

"What you really believe. What you hold within your heart. Will become yours. Isn't that the first tenet on perception in the manuscript?"

A smile. "It's on page one." Cashel raised the manuscript she had yet to put down, opening it to just the right page and began to read.

THE FIRST TENET

What you really believe. What you hold within your
heart. Will become yours.

Understand your thoughts, for thoughts create your
reality. You end up being what you think you are. You
end up getting what you think you shall. Thoughts are
created by imagination. Imagination is created by the
intentional expansion of mind. And mind is a magic
coupling of all the separate, unique, individual parts
that make up All That Is. You are one of those
wonderful, beautiful, individual separate parts.

Those thoughts, originated and controlled by you, and
then influenced by the energy around you, create your
reality.

Goble was pleased. "Now you might guess why I started on the path to see Tandara after you did and got here before you."

"My perception was different than yours. So my experience was different than yours."

"Exactly."

"My brother told me that my trip up the mountain was a long one. And a hard one. I forgot about the nice time I've always had climbing it. I let his thoughts influence my feelings about it which were much different."

"Yes. So you created a situation where his beliefs influenced who you were so much that they actually created your reality for you."

"Can we talk some more about the Hollows?"

"In a minute. What's the second tenet of *Gifts of Perception?*"

Cashel flipped through several pages before placing her hand in between to stop the pages from continuing their movement. She came to rest on the second tenet.

THE SECOND TENET

Survival doesn't exist. For all life is ongoing. There is no easy way. There is no hard way. There just is.

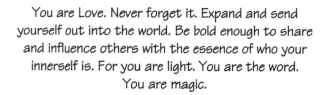

You are Love. Never forget it. Expand and send
yourself out into the world. Be bold enough to share
and influence others with the essence of who your
innerself is. For you are light. You are the word.
You are magic.

Cashel was smiling. From out of nowhere the
message had hit home. She had a fleeting thought
that Dragit would benefit from *Gifts of Perception*.
But she also understood that he needed to move
forward at his own pace. And, for some reason, he
was still asleep in one of the rooms of the house
rather than here with them, going over the various philosophical tenets that he also needed to
learn. At some point she would ask Tandara or
Goble about letting Dragit read the manuscript at
a later date.

But even as she had the thought, the answer
began surfacing within her. It was simple, really.
Tandara's way was that experience was the best
teacher. This was always the first lesson. And
experience usually came long before the actual
philosophy was to be presented and take root.
About the point she was at right now. With a

The Passage, the Gift, and the Prophecy

minor sigh she remembered back to her first experience.

She had been on the plateau less than an hour when she thought she heard some sounds coming from the old wooden well. Walking to the well, Cashel moved close enough to peer into what appeared to her to be an endless downward funnel.

"Hello down there. Can anyone hear me?"

Nothing.

"Hello. Is anyone down there?"

Still nothing. So she began walking away from the well. When she got within fifty feet of the house she heard the sounds again. Turning and walking back over to the well, she grabbed the bucket from its attached rope and began lowering it into its depth. Fifteen minutes later she was still in the process of lowering the bucket by unrolling the rope that wound around the beam above its opening.

"This doesn't make sense. This rope has no end. And my arm's getting tired. Every time it looks like I should be at the end of the rope, new rope appears. I've got better things to do with my time."

It was then that she heard it. A voice soothing and clear. But it wasn't the sound she had heard before, that had caused her to go over to the well in the first place. It was Tandara's voice. And it was coming from right behind her.

"The well has no bottom to it. Because the rope is part of the well it has to conform to the well's design. Therefore, the rope is endless."

Cashel turned slightly into the smiling, peaceful face of Tandara, her stare matching the magic in the old woman's eyes.

"The well is symbolic. It's a constant reminder to those that choose to interact with it, that all things are infinite and eternal. The comment you finally made out loud, about having better things to do with your time, is what drew you to the well in the first place. That feeling started as a thought within you. And in a way that you'll learn as we go along, you created the situation that would draw you to the well. It was so that you could experience, so that you could teach yourself first hand, that you really have as much time as you desire. For time, like the well, is infinite and eternal."

Cashel changed her mind. She wouldn't bother either Tandara or Goble with a question that had been forming in her mind, one that she now understood she already knew the answer to. That would have been giving her power away and she knew better than that. That had been another of the lessons that Tandara had taught her. Contain her energy. Don't disperse it. Focus it on what you already know. You'd never run out of it, for it is also endless and infinite. But never, never, disperse it uselessly.

Amazing how fast the mind channels information and analyzes it for the human brain. All of Cashel's thoughts took only seconds before she was brought back to the present by the sound of something awful. A screech or a scream. It wasn't clear. A howl or a shriek. It wasn't definable. A wail most likely but still indistinguishable. What was distinguishable was the sound of feet scurrying at a fast pace, hitting the floor one after the other, driving to reach their destination. And then suddenly, "Cashel! Cashel!!"

Rounding the corner of the room at a fairly swift pace was Dragit. "Cashel!!! Cashel!!!!"

Goble was the first to respond. "In here, Dragit. Just don't trip over the . . ."

It was too late. He was moving so fast that he failed to notice the coffee table directly in his path.

His body didn't. But rather than trip over it he slid into it, the coffee table magically parting to allow him to enter its space, and then closing on him, stopping Dragit right smack in the center of it. Cashel couldn't believe it, placing her hand on her mouth for fear of laughing and upsetting him even further. Goble just shook his head slowly from side to side and Tandara collapsed back into the chair she had been sitting in.

Wiggling and pushing against the table with all his might, Dragit was trying desperately to once again extricate himself from an impossible situation. "I don't understand this. How come I can't get out of here? And what's that horrible sound? I'm frightened. Cashel!" His body twisted and turned in every direction, but he was now part of an object that he couldn't release himself from. He was definitely stuck again. "Are one of you going to help me, or are you all going to just stand there?"

"Cashel, read to Dragit the third tenet from the manuscript. Let's see if he's learned anything and just needs to be reminded of it."

Silently reacting to Tandara's instructions, Cashel once again flipped through the manuscript, the pages coming to rest on tenet number three.

But before she could read, Dragit was on her. "How is listening to someone read something going to help me out of my predicament? I'm in the middle of a coffee table and I can't get loose."

THE THIRD TENET

Look to your inner guide to life's answers on your physical experience. Only by looking within will you begin to understand the mysteries you've so cleverly created and have chosen to solve.

Have a conversation with yourself often. Ask yourself many questions on the specifics of your life. Then simply remain silent and have the wisdom to listen to your inner voice. We can guide ourselves through all of life's obstacles with the knowledge contained within each of us.

Goble was patient, hoping that Dragit would realize what to do. But it wasn't yet to be so. "Cashel, let's try again. Find and read for your brother the next tenet."

Quickly, she turned the pages to locate the fourth tenet. But to no avail. "I can't find it."

"It's there, Cashel. Look harder."

Scanning and turning every page so that none were missed, it was becoming obvious that Cashel was focused on finding the tenet. But apparently to no avail. "I still can't find it."

"Cashel. Do you believe it's there?"

"I think so. But number six comes after number three. The fourth and fifth tenets are missing."

"If you believe it's so, that's the way it'll be."

Frustration colored her face. No matter how many times she moved the pages back and forth she couldn't locate the fourth tenet. Once again she was letting Dragit's frustration color her own knowing.

Tandara's soft melodious voice helped focus her concentration. "Stop a moment, take a deep breath, and think of a blank white screen. Got it?"

"Got it."

"What do you see?"

"The fourth tenet."

Both Tandara and Goble exchanged surprised smiles with Goble taking the lead. "What does it say?"

THE FOURTH TENET

Never doubt yourself or your own power.

Life is a series of events that we bring into our world
for the experience. There are always rewards for our
efforts.

Without anyone saying anything further, just as he had with the ground outside, Dragit closed his eyes and focused. He focused on seeing himself standing next to Cashel rather than in the middle of the coffee table. And in the magic of the moment, a second before the hail began hitting the plateau in a thundering force that began to rock the house and its inhabitants, he was free.

Chapter Four

The wind outside was picking up and the clouds were becoming darker. Tandara, Cashel, Goble, and Dragit had been talking for over an hour, both Tandara and Goble being very careful in how they explained just who the Hollows were, and what they were doing now ascending her mountain.

"Do you understand now why it's so very important to believe in yourself before they actually appear to us here?"

"Yes" was the only word Cashel was able to utter.

Dragit wasn't quite as definite. "I still don't think that that'll be enough. There's an army climbing up the mountain. There are only four of us. What happens if they drag all of us off the mountain? Then what? I suppose all we have to do is think them not here. Cashel, do you know what you got us into here. We may never get to go back down . . ."

"Oh Dragit, clam up. You're not helping and you're making me awful mad. I'm sorry I brought you with me now. Why is it so hard for you to be supportive? You know how the energy works up here. If you keep thinking the way you do, it's only going to get you into trouble when they get here. And no one's going to be able to help you but you. All you have to do is change your thinking. Get rid of your judgments of what's possible and what's not. Just think about the effect you want. Jeez . . ."

Tandara and Goble had captured the full attention of both of them as they related the story of the Hollows. To see Cashel, sitting on one of the chairs, eyes larger than normal, ears riveted to every word, lips gone dry, not moving an eyelash from her position, it was easy to see the love and admiration she had for Tandara and the growing sense of affinity with Goble.

Cashel thought she had an idea. "Tandara, before they reach the top is it possible to talk with

Palimar about any of this? I mean, he's a part of it also, isn't he?"

"Very much so. Everyone here on the plateau is a part of it."

"I know I'm not able to talk with him yet, but maybe with your help?"

For a split second before she said anything, Cashel thought Tandara was looking through her. Then she offered Cashel her thought. "How did you know that Palimar was able to talk?"

Cashel bowed her head slightly then looked up at Tandara with those wonderfully large eyes of hers and a half smile that said "I thought so."

"Why you stinker. You tricked me into telling you."

Twice now Dragit had opened his mouth to say something but had closed it just as quickly, not wanting to appear stupid. But the pressure was too much. "Who's this Palimar anyway and why will he only talk with you?"

Goble was becoming fond of Dragit. And in a way, Dragit's mistrust of what both Tandara and he had been saying endeared him to the boy even more. Intuitively he understood the boy's perspective. Especially at his age. If he had discovered Tandara and her magic at the same point in time he might have responded identically. He may have even been worse. "He's a very good friend of all of us, Dragit. He's Tandara's horse and actually, he'll talk with anyone who knows how to talk with him."

"Right. A horse that talks. Next you'll be telling me that somewhere up here there's an elephant that flies. . . . There's no horse up here. I would have seen him by now."

"There is indeed a horse up here, Dragit. Although you may not be able to see him the way you'd like too."

"What do you mean?"

"Goble, why don't you explain to Dragit about Palimar while I help Cashel with her wish." In a very tender way, Tandara took Cashel by the hand and walked over to the door. "In time you'll be able to talk to him on your own, without my help. All it will take is a change of perception on your part that all things are possible. But for right now I'll help you by allowing you to see a little more of the entire realm of things. Let's both of us concentrate on Palimar, telling him we'd like to talk with him and see if he comes over to us."

In her mind's eye, Cashel pictured herself and Palimar walking up the path to the plateau. She moved her thoughts to form a picture of Palimar following her, nudging her occasionally, walking along beside her and slowly turning from his nonphysical visual essence into a hard-bodied physical graphic. Tandara, unknown to Cashel, was joining her projection, adding her energy to the vision. She was helping by moving it in a direction away from them, high into the air, as if bouncing off the still life painting of a stationary star and then seeing the energy of its formation heading back down to the area of its general origination.

"I think we did it, look." From around one of the grassy knolls, Palimar was gently trotting toward them. His head held high in the air, with his silky mane gracefully moving in rhythm with the ever-thrashing winds of the mountaintop. As he moved toward them, the magic of the unknown was showing itself. From an outline of pure energy his form was becoming more and more physical, with the magic light of his being radiating in a circle around him rather than confined to the space of his energy presence. He was the most amazing color Cashel had ever seen. Several other times he had become physical for her, but the richness of his coat had never shown itself so beautifully. Like wonderfully laced marble, it was the color of golden chestnut, mounted on it an exceedingly long mane and matching tail, both a shade of cream with a look as smooth as silk. His size matched the largest of horses and was quite impressive, suggesting to those who gazed upon him a sense of true power. Even Goble, with his tall lean body, when standing next to Palimar seemed mighty small. But Palimar was a gentle giant and Cashel knew it.

Leaving them to their own devices, Tandara retreated back into the house. "Hello Palimar, you old wonderful creature you. I've missed you so much. Will you talk with me about the Hollows? I should be calm inside with everyone around, but a part of me feels like quivering jelly."

Palimar, always nurturing, gave Cashel a pleasing nudge and a neigh. Then, before her eyes she watched as Palimar took on an even sharper and deeper physical presence and then slowly, in the sweetest voice she had ever heard, begin to speak to her. The combination of being able to hear him, and the smooth rhythm and balanced cadence of his voice, began to make her tear ever so slowly.

"The Hollows are of concern to all of us. They are soulless spirits. They have been with the earth as long as its existence and before that in the minds of many. They live within themselves and bring an essence, a vibration, a frequency with them that is unpleasant for all who come in contact with them. They take away creative thought from the painter, inspiration from the musician, and light from the spiritual. It's their desire to control all thought rather than allow all creatures their freedom to manipulate matter into what they will, and create their own reality. With minor exceptions they don't look to win small battles with others. Their battlefield is the entire universe with all of its physical and nonphysical dimensions and realities."

Barely able to hear her own voice, Cashel needed to ask her question. "Tandara and you are two of those minor exceptions, aren't you?"

"Yes. As is now Goble. Through Tandara and his own wanting he has learned many of the secrets of creating in this physical sphere."

"Is Ginruss safe?"

"Yes, in a way. And yet in a way not. You see, both Ginruss and yourself . . . and Dragit . . . are still in a state of becoming. Still trying to learn about your powers and tap what you can. Because neither of you will be able to take an offensive posture against the Hollows, they won't be primarily concerned with you. On the other hand, because your beliefs about yourselves are not yet solidified within you, because they're still changing, they'll feel that you'll be the easiest to corrupt and give up your power."

"My power?"

"Yes. Your power. Ginruss' power. And Dragit's power. Remember what I said about the Hollows desire to contain and control your thoughts."

"My thoughts are mine. How can someone else take them?"

"By tricking you all into thinking that what you believe, what you know in your heart, is not so."

"How can they do that?"

"In the same way that your brothers and sisters tried to influence your thoughts about coming to see Tandara. In the same way that Dragit influenced your perception of the beauty you usually see when you climb the mountain to the plateau. By making you doubt what you already know."

"Tandara and Goble said that I have to stay focused on all the positive things I like, and not let negative thoughts enter my mind."

"They are indeed trying to help you to grow and maintain the wonderful innocence that you carry within you. You also must remember to use your imagination often, as you focus on the things that you want in your immediate future."

"They talked about that also. Tandara says that the more emotion I put behind thoughts of what I want, the more quickly I'll bring it to me."

Suddenly out of nowhere the ground began to move. Smooth gentle motions at first, like a wave of water under the ground moving in its rhythmic undulating motions, first side to side then back and forth. A small curling wave quietly rocking the grass and trees, animals and humans that stood upon it. The pleasant nurturing invisible hand of mother earth saying hello. Palimar was backing away from the entrance to the house where the two of them had been talking. But he wasn't backing away alone. Held tightly in his mouth was Cashel's arm. With each passing second, from the time the first wave had begun, Palimar had moved back a stride, within the first thirty seconds of the rolling wave an additional thirty paces from the house.

On the inside of the house, both Tandara and Goble had made their way with a somewhat frightened Dragit, to its center. Without hesitation, Tandara had led them into one of the three rooms in the center of the house, each room divided by a wall that the other shared, all coming together at a point in the center. Immediately on entering the room, a room Goble had never been in before, he stopped suddenly and just gazed at what appeared to him to be another outside area. The expanse was incredible. Far larger than the entire house would be able to contain, much less the tiny room they had entered, the space was the size of a small pasture. The grass however was not green. It was golden. And the sky was not blue. It was a wonderful light green hue. There was a sun in the sky also. Actually two of them. The larger one was about half the size of what he was used to seeing, and the smaller one half its size again. Both suns looked as if they had been bathed and dipped in a combination of the colors of peaches 'n' cream. As his eyes searched the landscape he noticed a great many animals freely roaming its surface. Animals of all shapes and sizes. Most he was familiar with. Some he was not. Some grazed, some seemed to play. Most kept to themselves. And the few who appeared thirsty, quenched that thirst in a lavishly forged spring, containing of all things, orange water.

If Goble showed surprised, it was nothing compared to the look on Dragit's face. Although he couldn't see all the changes in the landscape that Goble and Tandara could, the changes he could see, remained inconceivable to him. "Oh I get it now. I'm still asleep. This is all a dream. I'm going to wake up soon. I didn't really get lodged in the coffee table . . ."

"Yes you did," offered Goble.

"I'm losing it. This isn't supposed to happen until I'm as old as you."

"What do you think?" was all Tandara could think to say.

"It's beautiful," was a mouthful for Goble. But it would take some getting used to. "Everything is not as I'm used to seeing it. But then again, it's time for me to expand some more also."

"Dragit, how about you?"

"Everything's a different color here. The grass is kind of yellowish and the sky looks like it's green. Is that possible?"

"Did you hear that Goble? Improvement. Dragit is asking if it's possible rather than saying it's impossible. We're actually making strides here."

"Dragit, how many suns do you see in the sky?"

"What do you mean how many suns. One. One big one."

Goble was amused. "What color is it?"

"Yellow. What did you expect me to say, pink?"

Tandara was next. "What do you think of the spring, Dragit? The color I mean?"

"It's only water. It's . . . It's . . . It's changing. It's beginning to look . . . Orange?"

Goble just smiled over at Tandara as he hunched his shoulders, as if to say, "strange."

"We're moving forward in small steps, but at least we're moving forward," an amused Tandara returned.

"Are we safe in here? Wherever here is."

"Within this environment we're safe from the energy movements of the Hollows. And for awhile, Cashel and Palimar and Ginruss are quite safe where they are. The energy field over the top of the plateau will protect them from any intrusion beyond the top of the mountain, save the slight movements we were beginning to feel."

The lines of a furrow began to show on Goble's forehead and a serious side Tandara had not seen before, verbalized itself. "It's you they would most like. Maybe you should stay within these surroundings until their affront is discontinued. I'll go back out and see what I can do."

"Your thoughtfulness is genuine, dear friend, but you are not correct. They are here for both of us. Your abilities have become strong enough now that you have given them reason for concern. And before this day is over you'll find yourself having gained command of one additional skill, one that will concern them very much."

"Are you speaking of . . .

"Yes. The ability to move between varying realities in much the same way that Palimar does . . ."

Goble closed his eyes and thought for a moment. He had tried many times before to master moving between different realities. Each time he had failed. What was going to be different this time? Was this the real reason Tandara had sent for him? Was this his final lesson? For the first time in a long time, Goble felt a twinge of confusion and doubt. And it was sensed by Tandara.

"Goble my old friend, relax. I've suggested what I have to you, knowing your past attempts."

"But today of all days. This whole week has been one of forgetting my dominion and instead trying to control my events. We've already talked of that. Why the memory lapses? And with them what makes you think I'll master today what I've been unsuccessful at in the past?"

"Memory lapses are sometimes caused by energy surges within us, preparing us for additional growth. You're quite normal. And, the past is the past and today is today. You'll do fine. For now, just focus on what your next big forward movement is going to be, and remember, we're quite safe for now. As it is, a special shield began to immediately surround the house when the movements first started. We have as much protection as we need. As for the others, Palimar knows what to do to protect them if the need should arise. More than likely he has already moved Cashel and Ginruss far from the house to keep them away from the additional energy of the shield. If they had stayed within it, it would have strongly distorted their reality for a time. A complication that wasn't necessary for the moment."

On the outside of the house, on the grounds throughout the plateau, the movement was continuing. But Tandara's friends were nowhere in sight.

Palimar had taken the precautions Tandara had thought he would when the ground beneath them had started to roll. First, moving Cashel away from the additional energy field that was beginning to surround the house so that she wouldn't be harmed, and then instructing her to stand over by the tree stump where Ginruss was already located. He then went about gathering all the additional animals and also brought them over to the area of the stump. When all who normally roamed the plateau quite freely were assembled, he touched the pyramid-shaped crystal that was suspended several inches over the tree stump with his nose and neighed gently. At once the rainbow vibration that ordinarily covered the entire plateau reduced itself in size to cover only those surrounding the tree stump. Immediately, all holding their place began to feel the air thin and their skin or coat turn from the opaqueness that it was to a translucent blending of all around them. In essence, they were one with their surroundings. They were invisible to outside eyes.

At first Cashel was a little startled, but nothing compared to Ginruss who had curled up alongside of her, closer than her own skin. Cashel's eyes were big, but Ginruss' had exploded into moon-sized stars. He was very unsure of what was happening. Cashel, sensing his fear, moved her arm from the side of her body, placing it on the top of his back, mixing her fingers throughout his coat, reassuring him that everything was just fine and that Tandara and Palimar had everything under control. By helping to reassure Ginruss, she had cleared her mind of her own disruptive thoughts, eventually discovering for herself that she felt much better than she had originally.

All in all, the rolling motion of the surface ground lasted for quite awhile, but eventually gave way to the calm that surrounded the energy on the plateau. Everything was now still and once again peaceful.

But not for long. On the far side of the plateau, covered by the heavy mist that had been surrounding the mountain top, a form was beginning to show itself. Vague at first, but enriched very shortly by the electrical current that was shooting through it. Initially an enjoyable sight, but like all outer coatings its interior was about to show its true colors.

Our three inhabitants, not yet having released themselves from the tree stump or the rainbow vibration, had focused their vision on the figure. Because the other animals that Palimar had gathered around the stump were unfamiliar with the Hollows, their fear was not as noticeable as Ginruss' and Cashel's. Trying her best to keep her own thoughts in check and not allow them to influence Ginruss and the others, Cashel began putting a mental, pyramidal-type canopy over all of them. At the same time she began projecting a mental glass barrier in the direction of the ascending figure. For a moment she thought that she had failed, as the figure, now larger and more menacing than anything she had ever seen before, began to take its first step onto the plateau. But it wasn't to be.

As it placed what looked in appearance like a foot onto the flattened area of the top of the mountain, it faltered. First because of the normal vibrational energy of the plateau itself, and secondly because it immediately hit the invisible solid barrier that Cashel had envisioned. Instantly there were millions of electrical sparks flying in every direction around the figure, giving it the appearance of helplessness. But rather than forcing it away from its newly created border it only seemed to make it angry, its response to increase itself in size.

Cashel, unsure now of her ability to help, unwittingly withdrew her energy from the barrier she had created around the figure. The response was instantaneous. Although the figure was still unable to place its presence on the plateau itself, it was now able to lift its energy high into the air creating the most foreboding presence any of them had ever seen. Coupled with blasting winds that were now blanketing the plateau, and the highly audible sounds that they make, the experience was ominous.

It was now up to Palimar. As Cashel watched, Palimar became a shadow of what was left of him and then disappeared altogether. Cashel's heart felt as though it was going to leave her chest. Ginruss was frozen in place. Both had the feeling of helplessness, not really comprehending what had happened to Palimar. And a moment later, when the thunderous clap came from the skies above, the two of them sank as close to the ground as they could possibly get, hugging the grass below them, feeling that they were trying to imbed themselves as deeply into the mountain as they could.

In the skies above, another adventure was being played out. From Cashel's visual, she could make out an additional kind of electrical force beginning to surround the huge figure. In what appeared to be a very fast counterclockwise motion, spinning back and forth, crisscrossing its own repeated movement and then moving at right angles over its own path, this new electrical force was now the prominent player on stage. Seemingly, it was trying to cover all of the emptiness surrounding the earthbound electrical figure in such a way that not one additional particle of space could be breached, for no room would remain.

For a moment it looked as though it was working. And then, with a very powerful forward thrust, the figure moved out of not only the criss-crossed energy barrier surrounding it, but also projected who or whatever was providing it, far out into space. It was a defeat for Palimar. But not a deterrence. Looking down from a distance, Palimar understood that the energy vortex he had created had not held. He now knew that they could override a certain amount of his energy. He had simply miscalculated. This time he wouldn't.

From the invisible atomic structure he knew himself to be, Palimar began to become visible in as light a translucent state as he felt he could. Next he made the decision to enlarge his own visual and then expand the energy field he had just created, returning and reinforcing it at the same time. Then slowly, ever so slowly, he began to close its perimeter around the figure continuing to tighten his grip, squeezing his energy into the space the figure was occupying. Much like an eraser on a chalkboard, the once ominous figure of the original electrical form began to reduce itself in size, finally reaching and realizing a point within itself of too much compressed energy. The explosion was deafening. And the light show created from it was magnificent. But Palimar was not gloating. He understood all too well that you can never destroy energy, but rather simply displace it. The electrically charged form of a scout Hollow had simply decided to give up the space it was occupying, and return its energy to the position of its genesis before it had reached the mountaintop.

Chapter Five

Magus was not happy. He knew Tandara had become strong and had cultivated many friends, most of them very powerful themselves, but his scout had been rebuffed too easily. And for all the time it had taken him to rebuild his army and his strength after his last confrontation with Tandara, he wasn't going to give in easily. He would send another scout ahead to the plateau, this time targeting those not so strong. He would start there. Then the momentum would build.

If asked, not one of the Hollows would have been able to tell you just who Magus was or where he had come from. But they had all accepted him as their leader long ago. With an energy much heavier than any of the others, had he been allowed to have taken physical shape, he would have looked like an old, larger than life sea captain. On the top of his head was a dingy looking feathered hat covering his long dirty black hair. Below that you would have been able to make out an eye patch coating the skin just below his left eyebrow, while on another part of his face, the few teeth he had remaining were laminated with a thick coat of what looked like black tar. His beard was an identical match to the hair on the top of his head, long, black, and dirty. And the peg leg that would have normally appeared at the point in his physicality where his foot should have been, actually made up the greater portion of both his legs. He was mean. He was determined. He was the leader of the Hollows.

And, with his help and guidance they were now more than halfway up the mountain. He was still somewhat amazed at how long it had taken. It was like trying to move through Jell-O. And one area, the magical stream that flowed naturally uphill, that had been Goble's path to the mountaintop, had become an Achilles heel for them. They had learned the hard way to stay clear of the stream, understanding that each time they crossed its path, the energy that moved it against

The Passage, the Gift, and the Prophecy

the normal gravitational pull, would abruptly increase its intensity, interrupting its upward flow and then automatically reverse directions. What would follow, was a torrential rush of rapid-like waves of energy that would move them back downhill at an incredible speed, forcing them to begin again from the base of the mountain.

Magus had no idea just what corner of the universe his scout's energy had been dispersed to. He was very aware though, that it would take time for his energy to regain its center and regroup. When he did return, Magus would force him to maintain his focus within the invisible bars of energy they called solitude. He would not be allowed to communicate with any of the other Hollows nor they with him, until Magus made the decision to allow him to release himself. This was the price the scout would pay for failure to maintain his presence on the mountaintop. But for now, he had one less soldier to move against Tandara and her friends and this angered him.

As he assembled the chosen few from his small army he felt the necessity to explain to them. For they had never seen a more demanding Magus. Never one more focused in all of their time together and never more scheming. He knew he had used every trick he could muster, told every lie necessary, manipulated anyone who stood in his way. He had a goal. Nothing was going to stop him. He was out to destroy Tandara and her friends. But before their destruction, he was going to take back from them what had been taken from him.

Beginning softly and then moving quickly into a fevered dispatch, Magus made his statement to the chosen few of the Hollows. "There is only one way for this to end. A total and complete return to us of what is our natural birthright. What was taken from all of us a long time ago was not Tandara's to take. Our individual souls. The souls that once moved within us and shadowed our reality belong only to us. This emptiness within our spirits will not stand throughout time. We have returned for what is ours by natural right. First we will reclaim our entitlement, and then, complete annihilation of the energy sources that took it from us."

All was still and silent until one called Celone made her feelings known. And, although much like Magus, carrying a very heavy energy, her physicality, had she also been allowed to express it, would have produced a long and slender shell and a crop of lengthy golden hair. "Magus, I ask you again to reconsider this venture. The last time we approached Tandara we were defeated badly. Just as we have grown in strength over the pas-

The Passage, the Gift, and the Prophecy

sage of time, so has she. Another defeat will separate us for an even longer period of time. Possibly eons. There are other avenues open to us that hold a greater chance of success. We must be able to . . ."

The mighty roar of thunder and a barrage of accompanying energy bursts of spike-like pulsations, instantly focused their mass on surrounding those that had gathered to hear Magus' inflexible heart. To all of the Hollows these darts of fire were intimidating, magnetically and psychologically holding them in place, refusing them exit or leave. Even Celone was now seen cowering in response.

In time, everything returned to normal. Outside the house on the plateau the ground had stopped rolling and with one small exception, which was a thunderous booming clap of lightning, the electrical show in the sky above had suddenly ceased. Ginruss was to be found off in one of the corners back behind the house, digging up a mound of freshly planted wildflowers, but Palimar it seemed, had disappeared.

Within the house, Tandara, Goble, Cashel and Dragit, were each involved in their own undertaking. Cashel, off by herself, had been reviewing the manuscript and its messages.

THE FIFTH TENET

Growth comes by way of allowance of another person's touch.

Each experience begins an unending spiral throughout eternity of repeated experiences until the lesson is learned. Only then will the circle be closed to allow room for new growth and additional advancement.

Cashel wasn't sure where the music was coming from, but she loved it. It was soft and beautiful and allowed her to absorb the tenets in a different mental state. One free of worry and fear. The soothing melody that flowed throughout the house, seemed to echo within each room allowing her to focus on a never place and a never

The Passage, the Gift, and the Prophecy

thing, far from any type of physical reality her surroundings offered her at the moment. She found it fascinating, these sounds that filled her head. Never before had she been able to concentrate and understand so completely what she was learning. Every word, every sentence, every phrase of the tenets was finding a place within her heart.

Tandara and Dragit were to be found in the kitchen where she was showing him how to grow food without having to plant and sow. She would first take a seedling and place it in the center of a large standing circular copper form, by holding it in the palm of her hand and offering it to the heart of the structure. Immediately, invisible forces would seize the seedling from her and suspend it in space, equal distance between the arms of the form. She would then place a small round crystal underneath the seedling in a special spot on the copper. Within seconds a magical line of bluish white light would descend from somewhere in the heavens through the open-air ceiling, and with pinpoint accuracy would hit the small round crystal, causing it to send a rainbow around the circular copper form. In turn, emanations from the rainbow would direct themselves onto the seedling.

Jeff Gutterman

"I don't believe what I'm seeing," said guess who.

"Believe your eyes Dragit. And if they're not enough, reach out and touch the seedling and feel it grow in your hand."

Dragit did just that, reaching through the rainbow, placing his hand just below the seedling. He was now feeling the growth taking place as the seedling began expanding even more, finally beginning to turn orange and take on form from the green stalk that had proceeded it. Different than he had viewed it just a moment before, now moving out from its center, separating from itself into the space of self-realization. Within seconds Dragit found himself holding not one, but several full-size carrots.

Goble was to be found in the library, reviewing what appeared to be several very ancient books. Having to handle them with the utmost care, concern over their ability to withstand continued physical contact of any kind, he laid them very carefully on the coffee table. He then adjusted the lights surrounding the room in such a way that every other light was turned off, the ones remaining not focused directly onto the books. He was looking for something very special. He just wasn't sure what.

The Passage, the Gift, and the Prophecy

Back in the kitchen Tandara and Dragit were playing teacher and student, although the student was somewhat reluctant. "Now you try it, offered Tandara to Dragit.

"I can't do that. It's impossible. You're tricking me in some way."

"It's no trick Dragit. I'll do it again for you." And she did. First by closing her eyes and concentrating on what she wanted and then lightly releasing herself from the physical rules that surrounded her. Slowly she began to rise an inch or two above the wooden floor in the kitchen. Then she allowed her feet to move her body in an upward direction, only seconds passing before appearing in horizontal suspension, without anything appearing to hold her in the space she occupied. Then, smiling over at him, now even in height to Dragit's chest level, she returned to the position she occupied just before her experience.

It was Dragit's turn and he knew it. "I'm not sure I can do this."

"Sure you can. Close your eyes."

For the first time since ascending the mountain, Dragit followed her direction without much of an argument. With his eyes now closed he waited. And waited. But nothing was happening. So, with one eye open and the other closed he glanced at Tandara. "Cute, real cute."

"No peeking. Close your eyes. Now concentrate. Imagine yourself in the sky above looking back down at yourself standing here. Can you see that?"

"Yeah, and I look pretty stupid."

"Never mind how you look, can you feel any different?"

Silence. Sincere concentration. Then, "no."

"Dragit."

"Alright, alright. Yeah, I feel a little different."

"Okay. Now, from above, reach down and put your hand around your shoulder area and then pull yourself up off the floor."

Dragit felt nothing, so he had no idea it had worked. Again he opened one of his eyes and looked toward Tandara but this time he couldn't find her. Until he looked down. By that time it was too late. He hit the ground with a thud. "Ouch. That hurt!"

"I forgot to tell you to just lift yourself up a little way. You lifted yourself halfway to the ceiling."

"Thanks a lot. I should probably get upset with you, but I didn't even think it worked."

"Good, we're making progress. Now, let's try something a little different."

"Does Cashel know how to do this?"

The Passage, the Gift, and the Prophecy

"No, not yet. Cashel's growth has been in a different direction. Although we all share many things on one level, the changes we each go through are what allow each of us to develop the characteristics necessary to experience life to its fullest. Right now your sister is learning in the way she does best. She's reading."

"What was that book you gave her?"

"The manuscript is very old. It was written many thousands of years ago by a group of people whose connection to spirit was well-known and maintained. They remembered their beginning. Where they came from. And they wanted others to remember also. By writing down a few simple laws and having them passed from generation to generation, they felt they would be serving all people everywhere."

"What's in it?"

"Laws that talk about how to flow with life rather than trying to control it. That's what you've just done when you moved away from yourself and viewed what you wanted from a higher perspective."

"That doesn't make sense."

"It will Dragit, it will."

On the other side of the house, the well-lighted living room played host to Cashel. She was leaning against two large feathered pillows

Jeff Gutterman

placed strategically on one of the corners of one of the oversized Indian throw rugs. Fascinated with each passing page, she continued to study the manuscript. After reading each tenet at least twice, she would stop and try her best to absorb its meaning and try to understand just how it fit into her life. She was doing well until she came to the sixth tenet.

THE SIXTH TENET

Your eyes are an aspect of your physicality. Your intuitive awareness an aspect of your spirituality. When in direct competition for your perception, allow your inner light to be your guide.

With each passing moment we effect our eternal mark on each other. As such, we move forward or backward, depending upon our alignment to truth. View each encounter in a positive light, and all energy sent by you toward another will forge an endearing bond.

The tenet made her think of Dragit and how negative he was most of the time. As positive as she always tried to be, there were times when they were together that she wanted nothing more than to fit her small hands around his little neck and shake, all the while screaming "wake up." That made her wonder what kind of a mark she was leaving on him. Would her past words and actions benefit him at some time or had she wasted them. She turned the page and glanced at the seventh tenet.

THE SEVENTH TENET

Sometimes a straight line between your initial thought and its ultimate goal is not the fastest route to creation.

Give thought to the interruptions throughout your daily life. Accidents, no. Mistakes, no. Planned encounters, yes. Brought together through mutually magnetized energy on a neutral basis to enhance the creative process.

They all heard it. They neigh of a horse. A horse in extreme pain. The sound had a shrillness to it that sent shivers up and down everyone's spine. It was a race to see who could make it to the front door and out into the open first. Cashel, closest to the front door, wasn't able to outrun her brother who moved like someone possessed when he heard the sound. In midsentence, explaining to Tandara that he wasn't about to try walking through the wall to the other side, because he just knew he'd get stuck in the middle, the wail of the horse provided his excuse, and he immediately darted out of the kitchen into the living area toward the door that Cashel had just opened.

Coming toward her like a streak of lightning, Dragit was a little too fast, not squaring himself properly as he rounded the corner for the door. He hit the wall with a loud thud, imbedding himself half in and half out of it. Cashel stared at him in disbelief as did Tandara and Goble as they passed him on their way out the door.

They all heard it again. This time the sound was somewhat muffled but still very painful to listen to. And whoever was making it was in a great deal of anguish.

Cashel was the first to speak. "Where's Palimar? I don't see him anywhere."

"She's right," was Goble's confirmation as he looked over the plateau.

Again the sound. And again. Nothing any of them could do could invalidate what they were hearing and the impression it was leaving. It was a bad daydream that no one could awaken them from.

Cashel was crying, tears running down her face at a record pace while Goble tried to comfort her. Tandara looked as though she wasn't sure what to do and this frightened Cashel even more.

It seemed they had all forgotten Dragit, who, with arms and legs flailing in midair, one of each on either side of the wall, was so imbedded that he couldn't make a sound.

The shrill sounds now surrounding the plateau were hollow and tunnel-like, emitting minor echo's with each passing wind tone. And then suddenly, just as they had started, they stopped.

"Tandara, what's happened? Is that Palimar? What are they doing to him? Can't we help in some way?" Cashel sounded like an even smaller child with her questions, but they were a necessary release for her and both Tandara and Goble understood it.

"Cashel, you need to calm down. We don't know that it's Palimar. The Hollows are very good at manipulating others feelings. If that's what they're doing, they're doing it through sound. And they're trying very hard to make us think it's Palimar. Don't buy into it. Don't give your power away to them like that. You know Palimar is very strong. If they do have him, he's powerful enough to use their own energy against them. Trust in who you know him to be. No matter what happens."

Goble, still with his arm around Cashel, was glancing back toward the front door, witnessing the sight of the back half of a body moving rhythmically without any music, trying unsuccessfully to free itself from its semi-internment in the wall. Smiling and shaking his head, he excused himself from Cashel and Tandara and walked back over to the foot of the moat. "Dragit, you amaze me. You have the knowledge of how to free yourself from anything, but you won't use it. Now stop that silly kicking, be still for a moment, and try to remember what you've learned since you've been up here. I know you can't see me but I'm only several feet from you. Do what you've learned to come over to me."

Slowly Dragit calmed down and within seconds found himself free from the wall, standing knee-deep in the moat in front of Goble.

"Why didn't you tell me you were standing next to water?"

"Why didn't you ask?"

"I couldn't see anything. The only part of my head that was sticking out from the wall didn't have eyes on it."

"Close your eyes."

"Can I get out of the water first?"

"No, close your eyes."

Dragit obliged. "Okay, they're closed."

"Now ask me a question."

"Why am I standing in this stupid water?"

"No, not out loud. In your mind."

"How are you going to hear it if I . . ."

"Do it!"

Feeling silly and wet, Dragit wanted nothing else but to move out of the water of the moat onto the grass Goble was standing on, so once again he followed the directions he was given. "Well, I did it, now what?"

"I didn't hear you."

"I know. How could you hear me if I wasn't saying anything?"

"Were you thinking about me when you asked me the question?"

"Why do I have to think about you? You're standing right in front of me . . . Alright, alright."

Dragit concentrated on his question, and in directing it toward Goble.

"Good, I got it."

"I'll just bet. What did I ask?"

"You wanted to know where the lamb was? And yes, you can close your mouth."

"How did you know?"

"I just listened very carefully. In time, if you want too, you'll learn how to listen also. Now you can climb out of the moat."

Tandara and Cashel had just approached Goble as Dragit was putting his feet on solid ground. Tandara gave him one of those looks, Goble just smiled and Cashel shook her head from side to side.

"Sometimes I find it hard to believe we're related. You've always got to learn the hard way."

"Don't be too hard on him Cashel. His lessons will settle with him when he's ready, as they do for all of us. Sometimes we allow ourselves to forget that this is an open-ended journey. The experiences, sometimes duplicated many times, are ongoing and endless. It's life. On either side of the veil."

Cashel was the first to enter the house, Tandara a step or two behind her, Dragit next with Goble bringing up the rear. After just a few steps all three could hear a splash behind Dragit.

The first to turn, Dragit couldn't believe his eyes. Immediately behind him Goble had sunk knee-high into the moat.

"And you were teaching me!"

"I can't believe this has happened to me again," was all any of them could hear Goble mumble.

Dragit wasn't going to miss a beat. "Close your eyes."

"What?"

"You want to get out of there, don't you?"

Silently shaking his head up and down, Goble did as he was instructed.

"Now concentrate on walking on top of the water, not in it."

Just before he rose up over the water line of the moat, Tandara noticed an almost imperceptible compression of Goble's lips. He was smiling the smile of a teacher that had just received his greatest reward. The student was teaching the teacher.

Chapter Six

THE EIGHTH TENET

The stepping stone to creation is action.
Without it, all thought will dwindle and die.

Fire your thoughts with passion, which by its very
nature requires movement. Stagnation will
not allow you your goal. Only a steady stream
of motion. Any kind of motion.

> For even if the wrong fork in the road is chosen,
> corrections cannot be made if
> forward movement hasn't begun.

Dragit was reading from the manuscript Cashel had laid to the side before she had fallen asleep. He had unwittingly opened it to the eighth tenet. Not quite sure he understood the meaning of the words he was reading he stood up, put his hands behind his back, one palm clasped into the other, and started pacing. Every once in a while he'd stop and move his head up towards the ceiling, pushing his lips together, as though he were contemplating the genesis of life itself.

Tandara on the other hand, had taken Goble back into one of the inner rooms that once again allowed them to find themselves on the outside in a completely different reality.

The first thing Goble noticed this second time was the music. It took him back, reminding him of his childhood and how he always longed to go off by himself. He used to enjoy thoroughly the beauty of everything around him, talking to trees and plants in the same manner he would another child. He shared with them his feelings, his joys,

The Passage, the Gift, and the Prophecy

and his heartbreaks. He seemed to know instinctively that they were his friends.

"Tandara, this music. It's doing strange things to me. It's the most ethereal music I've ever heard."

"Yes, I agree. No instruments of any kind. It's quite natural actually. What you're hearing is energy riding the puffs of air current, moving through the spheres. It's really very natural, and peacefully beautiful. But I moved us into this inner sanctum for a reason."

"And that is?"

"To help you complete your journey this time around. So allow the music to both relax and heighten your inner senses and listen carefully to what I have to say. In order for you to be able to move between dimensions, you need to be able to leave this one. And to do that, it's necessary for you to be completely in touch with who you really are. That means accepting all that has gone before as a part of yourself. To do that you must take time to discover who you really are. And then you acknowledge and, if necessary, forgive those hidden aspects of yourself that you haven't wanted to look at. You see, what held you back from success last time was your fear of self-approval and deservedness. In short, you need to

Jeff Gutterman

accept yourself totally to be able to enter and function in all realities."

"So what you're saying, is that my inability to look at portions of myself was what had to be overcome, because they didn't quite fit with who I was or wanted to be at any given moment. It makes sense. There are areas of my life that I've intentionally forgotten. Certain points in my past that were too painful to remember. That's why I always chose to go off alone when I was a child. When I was alone, away from everyone, I felt free and accepting of myself. Nothing to be a part of, no one to respond to. It was safer."

"Yes, it was safer. At least that was your perception at the time. But you know that anytime we're not totally accepting of ourselves, that part that we're not accommodating, dies a little. And when an aspect of ourselves dies, it makes it difficult for us to totally be here in the now. It means we're not living life in all its fullness, with all its riches."

"I think I see now why I'm so attracted to Dragit. He reminds me a great deal of myself when I was his age."

Tandara just smiled. "We each act as a mirror for others to gaze into and see themselves. The familiar qualities. The good ones, and those that are not always so comfortable to look at. And many times, without our understanding it, those mirrors, those reflections, take us back to another time that we've chosen to put far behind us."

"Where is the music coming from?"

"Another realm. If you listen for a few moments it'll help you return to an aspect of your past where you left a little piece of yourself. Now's the time to find it and retrieve it. Make it a part of you once again. Once you do that you'll find it very easy to move from one point to another, through any kind of invisible barrier, for any reason you choose. Cashel and Dragit are about to need my help, so I'll leave you, dear friend, to experience more of yourself." And with that Tandara walked back over to the door that the two of them had come through moments before, turned and threw a smile toward Goble and then turned again and walked through it.

The sky outside was losing its brightness, twilight, the entrance to evening, approaching quickly. To both Dragit and Cashel, viewing the plateau through one of the clear but wavy glass front windows, the day had been a short one. Quietly searching the grounds, neither one could find Ginruss, and Cashel, contrary to her resolution, kept trying to catch a glimpse of her special horse.

Tandara, standing back from the two of them sensed their feeling, and, approaching from behind, put an arm over each. Cashel was the first to turn and look up at her.

"We're closing on the end of the day, and quite a day at that. It's passed us by pretty quickly though, hasn't it? If you both feel like it, you can help me set the candles that Goble had taken from the shelf into their special places."

Dragit's interest was now sparked. "Where is he?"

"Goble is centering himself."

"Can I help him, whatever that means?" Dragit inquired.

"Centering is something we each have to do on our own. Although your offer is admirable, the only help Goble is allowed is what surfaces from deep down inside himself."

Dragit wasn't satisfied. What he needed were a few more answers. "What does it mean to center yourself?"

"To find a balance within yourself. To equalize your emotions, not giving any one of them more power over you than any other one. Not being more sad than you are happy. But being both equally. Not being more fearful than you are loving. Being both equally. Not just understanding but also feeling that no one emotional aspect of you is more powerful than any other aspect."

"Why is it necessary to do that?" whispered a tired Cashel.

"By balancing your emotions and centering yourself, you flow freely with the energy of your being. That allows you to manipulate physical matter to your benefit and to hear another person's thoughts when you're silent."

Cashel was alert. "You mean like being able to lay on top of water rather than sinking in it?"

"Yes, that's one of the ways to manipulate matter."

"That's why Goble could hear my question when I didn't say anything."

"Yes, that's exactly why."

"But that means that he was already centered if he could do that," came the voice of a confused Dragit.

"Yes, he was already centered. But there were still some things Goble needed to work on to be more so. To allow him to do several other things. That's what he's doing now."

The inquisitiveness in Dragit's voice was almost like an interrogation. "What other things?"

"Those other things are private to him just as you'll have some things come up that will be private to you. The choice of whether to share them with you will have to come from Goble himself. Now, let's find the box that contains the candles and do with them what we need to."

They moved from the living room into the library, Cashel in the lead followed by Dragit and then Tandara. A step or two into the new area was all it took for Cashel to come to an abrupt halt, Dragit immediately bumping into her and Tandara into Dragit. A quick glance about the room and it was easy to see why Cashel had stopped so suddenly. The books that normally lined the walls of the room were in scattered disarray. Several hundred, all sizes and shapes, lay sprinkled on the floor, some opened, some closed. From the sight of some of the open ones it was apparent that a number of them had lost much of their insides. In clusters on the floor, a good eye could see that some of the pages that had been ripped from the books laid alone, dispersed to all corners of the room. It looked nothing like the neat orderly chamber of archives that it was.

"Oh my," was the only sound to escape Tandara's lips.

All three of them continued to search the room, their eyes eventually falling on one little white four-legged bundle, huddled behind one of the tall lamps that surrounded the room. Ginruss was freely trying to smile up at them as he continued to hold his jaws together, clamped over one of the smaller sized books. As Cashel turned to Tandara for some kind of an answer, all Tandara could do was to hunch her shoulders in bewilderment.

"Ginruss, how could you do this? Tandara's going to have you for dinner . . . How'd he get in here anyway?"

"I have a feeling he doesn't know himself. Besides, he's not the problem. Even if he was able to reach some of the lower books he never would have been able to reach those higher than himself."

Dragit, sensing necessity, had begun looking for the box that contained the candles. Finding the box in a corner of the library, it lay on its side, several of the seven white thin candles themselves already exposed on the floor. Picking them up and returning them to their proper place, Dragit stopped to examine them more carefully than he had on first glance.

Noticing the whitish blue wick as it wound around the candle from top to bottom he held one out for Cashel to view. "I've never seen a candle like this before. Where did these come from?"

Tandara, still taking in the new essence of the room, had focused almost immediately on something neither of them had seen when they entered. Directly over the three large oversized chairs were three ancient books floating in midair just above the bottom cushions, one book per cushion. Had either Cashel or Dragit been able to sense Tandara's alarm, they would have been frightened. Releasing an inner emanation of tenseness she smiled and refocused on the two.

"So you found the candles. They're special Cashel. Friends of mine from long ago made them for me. Each candle will hold a flame indefinitely contrary to the thinness of the candle itself. Several times over the years that have passed they've been used when it became necessary."

Both Cashel and Dragit spoke at the same time. "What do they do?"

"They bring into each area they become a part of a very strong and necessary nourishment. In a way, the flame they emit enhances itself many times beyond what you see as its physical boundary. You could say that it's the food of life itself. Now, if you'll each help me, we need to locate the center of each room and then pace off seven feet north. We can start with this one. Dragit, first, you'll need to find the center, which in this room should be the middle of the coffee table, and then move seven steps to the north."

"How do I know which way is north?"

"The front door of the house faces north."

"Okay, I've got it, now what?"

"Hold the candle three feet from the floor, straight up, and let go."

Dragit did as he was told and much like the seed he had learned with in the kitchen, the candle stood by itself, floating in open space, three feet above the library floor. When he finished, Cashel offered to be responsible for lighting it.

"Not just yet, but when we're ready I'll show you how and you can do it."

In each of the outer rooms the process was repeated, Dragit and Cashel taking turns placing the candles, while a musical note that was Ginruss' bell, followed them wherever they went. For each of the three interior rooms the candle was placed just outside its entering door, centered at its entrance, also suspended three feet above the surrounding hallway floor. When all seven candles had been placed in their proper places, both Cashel and Dragit were led back to the outside of one of the interior rooms.

As she moved her hand in front of the door, shoulder height, in a half circular left-to-right motion, the door to the meditation room opened. All three, with Ginruss in tow, were able to bypass the suspended candle to enter the room.

Once inside, Dragit moved to its center and turned his body in a circle to review the room. He then looked over to Tandara and whispered, "Isn't this the room you took me into before?"

Whispering back she said, "Yes Dragit, the same one. By the way, we don't have to whisper."

"Okay, where's the bed that I slept on?"

"It's still here, in the same place you first saw it."

Dragit was confused. As his eyes searched the room he couldn't find the bed anywhere. For the first time, the room struck him as a small chamber. Within the room, touching a part of each side wall was a multifaceted circular white frame, several inches thick. The uniqueness of the frame was that it was made of nothing solid but rather what appeared to be a very dull, cream-colored light. Within the frame was a suspended pyramid made out of the same lifeless cream-colored light. With the depths of its sides exceeding the limits of the floor, the intimation was a stairway to its foundation. A foundation that was impossible to see. But as you approached it the illusion faded into two copper, side by side poles on the outside of the pyramids perimeter. To move from the outside of the poles to their inside, you would pass through an almost invisible, extremely thin sheet of water. What was magical about it was that it seemed to fluctuate in height depending upon the height of the individual that walked through it.

"I don't see it anywhere."

"Cashel, why don't you explain where the bed is to Dragit."

"Okay. It's just where you saw it the first time."

"Just when I was beginning to trust you guys."

"Nothing's changed, little brother, except your perception."

"When I brought you in here earlier, Dragit, you were very tired. You expected to see a bed in here. And so you saw what you expected to see by creating it for yourself."

"Remember when we were coming up the mountain I told you that this was a magical place," reminded a soft spoken Cashel. The energy works the same way here that it does down in our valley but much faster. If you think something then you get it real quick up here."

"Focus on the bed, Dragit, and you'll see it."

Dragit did as he was told, closing his eyes and holding an image of the bed he had slept in. When he opened them he could see it's almost indistinct outline within the pyramid, located where the bottom of the floor would normally be found, without the newly formed physical recession made by the sides of the pyramid.

"Well, I'll be a . . ."

Cashel was on him. "Dragit!"

"I was only going to say . . ."

"Dragit!"

"Alright, alright."

Tandara was almost laughing, but there was work to do. "If you'll both follow my lead please," whereupon she walked over to the two copper poles and slowly moved through them into the thin sheet of water and disappeared.

Dragit was the first to voice his opinion. "You go first."

"I don't mind doing that but why don't you want to go first?"

"I'm not real crazy about disappearing."

"What makes you think you're going to disappear?"

"I know what I see. Tandara just walked through that thing and disappeared."

Cashel was thinking of one of the tenets, she just couldn't remember which one. "Dragit, don't believe all you see. A moment ago you couldn't see your bed until you changed your perception. And now you know it didn't disappear. It was how you were viewing it. The same is true for Tandara. She hasn't disappeared. Now, am I going first or do you want to lead?"

That's all it took. A twinge of psychology. Dragit moved to the copper poles and, just as Tandara before him, walked through them.

Cashel was right behind. Passing through the sheet of water, Tandara was directly in front of him, glancing down, smiling her smile.

"How do you feel?"

"Okay. How should I feel?"

Tandara glanced toward where the top of the pyramid should have been. Dragit's eyes immediately followed her lead. An instant later, what had just happened registered with him.

"Oh my God! We're underwater," whereupon he started to gasp for air.

"It's okay Dragit, you can breathe down here, really."

He seemed to be making some kind of gurgling noise with a voice that had become indistinguishable. Cashel, who herself had just cleared the outside sheet of water with Ginruss and his musical bell, took a moment to sense what was going on and then tried to hold her laughter in. Remembering her first time, she felt a real affinity with what was happening and found herself leaning into him to try and catch something of what he was saying.

"I can't swim! I can't swim! Can you hear me, I can't swim!"

Cashel made a sign that she wasn't quite sure what he was saying and again leaned into him.

"If I can't swim then I can't breathe underwater! This isn't funny Cashel!"

And then he heard it. Goble's voice inside his head.

"Stop your thrashing around. You can breathe underwater. Do it!"

And he did. Exchanging glances between the water line above with Cashel and Tandara, he slowly began shaking his head that he was okay. But the lines on his young forehead had taken on the appearance of a ruffled brow.

"How come I could just hear Goble talking to me. He didn't come with us . . . wait a minute . . . I just realized something."

"What's that Dragit."

"None of us are moving our mouths to talk."

"I've been here before Dragit. Tandara brought me into the meditation room my first time here. Isn't it wonderful. We can hear each other's voice without any of us talking out loud."

"This is a real strange place. I can't even hear Ginruss' bell anymore."

"It's time to light the candles. Both of you form a circle with me and concentrate on the candles exploding into light."

Within seconds, the seven candles that had been carefully placed throughout the house, that were now well out of their range of vision, exploded with a wonderful luminescence. That was immediately followed by the circular white frame and the suspended pyramid within in it, losing its dull cream color and erupting into a brilliant pulsating beam of golden white light.

Chapter Seven

The Hollows had not been idle. On the side of the mountain one of the scouts had discovered a large cave. Fueled with mischief, the information had been returned to Magus who had decided upon a way to enhance their mission, and cause additional anguish to Tandara and her group before the actual war between them really began.

Summoning all the Hollows together, their spirits entered the cave. Long and slender, they found that it twisted and turned in many directions within the mountain's belly. Its purpose was unknown to any of them, but it mattered little. It would be used in alignment with their own objectives.

With Magus off to one side attending to another matter, Celone led the group of soulless spirits through the innermost bowels of the cave. Forging their way through at a faster and faster pace, they were unable to find its ending point. First they had ascended what seemed like twice the journey they had already come, and then, reaching what appeared to be a peak in their travels, began descending. All were confused at where they were being led, including Celone at the head of the group, guided always by Magus' thought, but none of them doubted what they were doing.

The energy pattern they were laying within the mountain was an unpleasant one. Filled with doubts and fear, and in turn loaded with their effects of negativity, anything that was alive within the long slender artery of the path they were traveling on died immediately. Nothing their energy touched stayed alive. Moss that was growing on the side of the cave's floor, turned a crisp yellow from its luscious green hue and then in turn the darkest black, ending its nature and existence as moss. Beginning life forms, moving in the tiny stream that ran the length of the cave's floor, ceased their excitement at movement and growth, curled into indistinguishable ameba, and faded from grace to become dust in the water.

"Celone, where are we headed? We keep moving, but we're going nowhere. Where is Magus leading us?"

"It's his decision that we continue to go forward, infecting this cave and its path with as much of our energy as possible. None of us need disappoint him."

But in her own mind, she wanted to stop what she was doing and withdraw from where Magus was taking them. Something within her knew there was disaster waiting for them on the plateau. And whatever it was would take from them even more of themselves than it had last time. Even the capture and transformation of the horse wasn't going to help them. She hated Tandara for what she had done to all of them. Especially to her. Tandara was never the sister to her that she was supposed to be. Identically born, but psychologically very, very different.

Goble was feeling lighter than air. Standing with his arms held away from his body, a horizontal line even with the ground he stood upon, he began to spin in a clockwise direction. Slowly at first, increasing the speed of each cycle with each turn. Faintly he began to mentally see himself disappear and then abruptly began to feel the structure of his illusionary body break into millions of tiny pulsating configurations. The atoms of the universe, moving and spinning within themselves and around each other, now at a much faster pace than his physical body would be able to harbor and hold together. Goble was becoming almost invisible and in so doing was closer than ever before in accomplishing what he had failed to the last time.

Long before he began his spin he had been in a meditative state for several hours, focusing on his past, bringing up what had been buried so long ago. When he first realized what he was seeing he disowned it, refusing to believe. He would come out and then go back into his meditative state many times. When he jarred himself loose from his vision he would cry and in his tears would find his voice. "No, no, this can't have been me."

But each time he moved away from his vision he would force himself back into it, knowing that the longer he stayed with it the more information he was being given, and in turn the more accepting he became. He remembered back when his disenchantment had begun, long before this lifetime. He was angry, and had been for many eons of time. He refused to take responsibility for himself, always blaming others for his problems, never quite seeing how he and only he created them himself. He was angry enough, that he wasn't projecting any positive emotion out into the world. And because he didn't use what had been given to him to make him whole, it was taken from him. He had become a Hollow. But not just a soulless spirit. He had become the leader of the Hollows. Wandering the emptiness of space, never quite accepting himself or others, he caused many problems for those he thought had wronged him. And with each minor defeat for another, he unknowingly kept defeating himself.

Until one day something began stirring within him. Something that said that what he had been feeling in the midst of his spirit, had been wrong and misguided. That was the first step for him in returning to himself, his whole identity, recapturing his soul within his spirit. Once the understanding had been allowed to seat within him and a decision had been made by him to try to reverse what had gone before, his vibration had begun to change, speeding up, and then over time, allowing him to accept the return of his soul.

It had been hard on him, reviewing this part of his past. But, as Tandara had said, necessary. At the point he was at now he could accept his past actions. He had not been strong enough and would not have been able to when he had first met Tandara. Knowing this and fully accepting who he was then and the fullness of who he had become today, he began to raise his arms up from the side of his body and move in a clockwise rotation.

THE NINTH TENET

If you choose positive projections for your
thought patterns,
you will continually surround yourself within an
attitude of Love.

Focus on yourself and your future.
Choose wisely to make it rightfor you,
and then allow the flow of energy from your center
to spread outward, moving you forward, seducing
others to sense and gather your strength,
thereby enhancing their own.

It was wonderful. In the meditation room Cashel was able to see the ninth tenet in her mind, as if written across a vast light blue sky when the melody of emotions was passive. "So clear," she thought. "So undisturbed." She was laughing at herself, entranced by what she was able to see without really seeing it. She allowed a momentary thought to move through her screen of vision, wondering if Tandara and Dragit were also receiving what they wanted with such impressive clarity.

Both Tandara and Dragit were also in their own meditative states, each receiving something different and supportive for their efforts. Tandara's focus was very determined, aligning her with the movement of the energy on the outside of her mountain. She would allow herself to inwardly view the whole of what was happening, but would not allow herself to cross over a very thinly veiled line of reading and entering the thoughts of the Hollows. Although she was both capable and powerful enough to do so, she knew that to invade a negative energy source such as the Hollows, her positive energy would have to momentarily blend and mix with theirs, granting them an excess of power they didn't need. For the moment she'd remain content, simply backing up and viewing the entire canvas.

Dragit on the other hand was doing something rather unusual. He was searching for answers. First, with his eyes closed, he focused intently on Ginruss, watching him move about within their underwater chamber. He could see the tiny round ball within Ginruss' bell moving this way and that, every fractured second clinging to the inside of the dome-shaped metal encasement itself. He was amazed at how he could either slow down the movement that was occurring within his mind's eye or speed it up. But what most surprised him, was his ability to perceive sound in a way he had not been able to since entering this submerged area of the meditation room. Everything was happening within him, not outside of himself.

Next, Dragit tried to bring what he had never seen into view. Concentrating and consolidating his thoughts, he imagined a white blank screen in front of him. Then he saw himself on the screen calling out to Palimar. What seemed like an eternity passed before he felt a sign of any kind that he was even on the right track. But then it happened. Before his mental eyes he began feel the energy of the outline of a very large figure. But it refused to take shape for him.

He tried calling out to him again. "Palimar, it's Dragit, Cashel's brother. I'd like to talk to you.

Please. I want to help. I just don't know how. Please Palimar."

Bits and pieces, but nothing concrete. He was frustrated so he tried once more. With all his will he tried calling to his new friend Goble. Goble was the one person that had proven to him that he could communicate without talking.

"Goble I need help. I'm trying to reach Palimar but he doesn't answer me. What have I done wrong?"

Silence. The passage of an eternity. Then, from Goble's wonderful calm voice. "Don't press for the answers you seek. Everything happens in its own time and for its own reason."

At almost the same moment all three opened their physical eyes. And before any of them could blink, the disorientation from their deep, meditative state, dissolved itself. Tandara then waved her hands and all four of them, Cashel, Dragit, Ginruss, and herself were standing back in the living room with Goble.

"How'd you do that one?" was Dragit's cry.

Goble smiled over at Tandara. "He still asks how life exists as it does."

"Yes my old friend. But he's learning very fast and for that we need to congratulate him."

"Cashel, in the kitchen there's a special drink I made awhile ago for all of us. Would you mind getting it?"

"I'd love to if you'll answer just one question for me."

Without waiting for the question Dragit blurted out the answer. "It's sunny outside because we were in the meditation room for a long, long time."

Tandara looked down at Dragit and even she registered surprise. "Very good, Dragit. He's right, Cashel. Physical time has moved forward for us while we were suspended in nontime. Actually many hours have passed."

Dragit's head was held high as he made his way out of the house with Ginruss. Cashel on the other hand, accepting as usual, moved toward the kitchen for the special drink.

When they were alone Goble glanced toward Tandara with wonder. "How long have you known?"

"Always."

"You never said anything."

"Would it have served you if I had?"

"No. You were right to maintain your silence. Thank you."

"Goble, that expression on your face. It's more of a frown. I'm not used to that. You came very close to succeeding at what you wanted. The next time will be even closer. This should be a time for celebration."

"Yes, I'm very pleased with the last couple of hours. That's not what's troubling me."

Tandara, trying to read her old friend, found it difficult. "I'm missing something, yes?"

With a wave of his hand he motioned her to follow him into the library. The room hadn't changed since she had last seen it. With a second gesture of his hand, Goble directed Tandara's vision toward the three floating books suspended over the three chairs surrounding the coffee table.

"Yes, I know. It seems the room has been breached in some way."

"I believe it's more than that. When I entered this area many hours ago I pulled four very ancient books from the shelves. Three of them you see before you. The fourth is missing."

Now Tandara was showing some concern. Looking over at Goble she started to speak, but again, with a wave of his hand asking for her patience, she acquiesced and allowed him to continue.

"I was searching for something, but I hadn't a clue as to what. Not the slightest idea actually. That is until I spent the time reviewing my past and learning how to completely let go of the physical, scattering myself to the far corners of space. As I began to regroup into physical form the answer came to me. Within the fourth book was a . . ."

The explosion was the loudest and most powerful yet. It shook the top of the mountain in such a way that the sound waves began moving in two opposing directions, giving one the impression of a tuning fork having just been lifted from its passive surroundings, turned upside down and banged against the side of a table.

The plateau began shaking like never before. Tandara now understood what the Hollows had been doing in the tunnel. It was as though they had loaded it with the most combustible item in the universe, setting it all off at once. As all three raced outside, Tandara and Goble from the living room area, and Cashel from the kitchen, two things were becoming very apparent. The first, although devastating, was the easiest to accept. The magical plateau was beginning to fracture, obvious by the newly formed and ever-widening crack that began on one side of the plateau and ran in a jagged line all the way over to the other side, missing the old well, the tree stump holding the crystal pyramid and the house by inches.

The second reality was a nightmare. Overhead in the daylight sky was the largest electrical dis-

The Passage, the Gift, and the Prophecy

play any of them had ever seen. Outlined in the midst of a flashing golden fireball were a million bolts of intensified lightning in the form of Palimar, larger than even Tandara had seen him before. As the figure neighed down on them in a voice both barren and boisterous it became very apparent that this was not the Palimar any of them had known and come to love. By all appearances this mild giant of a horse had switched sides.

Cashel was heartbroken. "Palimar, how could you? We all loved you so much. I loved you so much. How can you do this to Tandara?"

"Leave him be child. He's made his choice. There's nothing any of us can do now."

"I hate him. I just hate him," cried an angry Cashel.

Dragit was in awe. Never in his life had he seen anything so big and powerful. Now he understood why he couldn't reach Palimar when he had attempted to in the meditation chamber. He couldn't believe that this was the animal that Cashel had become so fond of and had talked for so many hours about. But at the same time that he was trying to make sense of it all, fear was gripping his soul. Palimar's long drawn out snorting was becoming louder and louder, coinciding quite well with the shaking and swaying of the plateau, which seemed to be throwing everything not tied down to something, from one side of the plateau to the other.

Tandara calmed her mind and concentrated intently on what needed to be done. With great intensity she focused the energy of her thoughts on the three invisible glass shields placed at various locations around the perimeter of the mountaintop. Within seconds, a fire-like rope, many feet thick, darted from the first shield to the second at the front of the plateau, and then stretching and reaching beyond the back of the house shot out to its sister shield, forming the third point of yet another pyramid. Having a girth exceeding the height of the house the energy of the fire-like rope worked quickly to calm the movement on top of the mountain, bringing to a halt the ever-widening fissure being created by the Hollows. Coupled with the form of Palimar dissolving into space the moment the form of the pyramid emerged, Tandara had restored momentary peace to her home and its inhabitants.

Chapter Eight

The sun and moon had exchanged places in the sky six times. This was now the morning of the seventh day. The fire-like rope still glowed, continuing to magically hold the top of the mountain together, keeping the plateau from splitting apart, creating two separate smaller mountains.

Many times over the last six days the Hollows had tried to breach the plateau, several times coming within an arm's length of the illuminated band that was the fire-like rope, only to be turned back by its brilliance. The radiating light was not something that they had counted on. Each time one of them had attempted to move through it or over it, a solid musical note would sound, shattering whatever part of their energy that had touched it. This had sent them back over the side screeching in pain, having had their essence touched by its innermost cord. Never before had they felt such disharmony within themselves.

Ginruss, on the outside, now on top of one of the grass mounds, watched with interest and a feeling of safety, moving his head this way and that, clanging his small bell each time one of the Hollows tried in vain to breach the plateau where he played.

Inside the house there was quiet. The energy in all the rooms had settled and balanced itself because of the embrace of the candles. Even within the library where the three ancient books still floated lazily above the chairs, the feeling was one of peacefulness and safety. But it had been a tense six days, none of them sleeping the sleep of a small baby. Tandara and Cashel shared Tandara's large bed in her bedroom, while both Goble and Dragit maintained their restless sleep states in the meditation room, where two beds had replaced Dragit's original one. And although both Cashel and Dragit had given thought to saying their good-byes to Tandara and Goble and returning to the calm and peacefulness of their village below, both understood that until the Hollows were put to rest once and for all, they would all remain prisoners of the plateau.

Tandara it seemed, was existing in multiple spaces, located within two completely separate universes, constantly dividing herself each time she fell into a sleep state. As necessary as it was to maintain her attachment to her physical surroundings while she explored her inner separations, it was also critical that she intuitively manage an overall awareness of the Hollows for as long as they remained on her mountain. It was easier in her sleep state but necessary in her waking state. She was living in two different worlds at the same time. Manipulating herself in this fashion was very tiring, displaying itself as it did with lines of concern converging on certain portions of her face, something Cashel had not seen before.

When Cashel had asked her about it, Tandara had simply said that it was necessary for the moment, but she felt that the Hollows would be gone soon and she would be able to retain more of her true energy. Besides, she was waiting for an old friend to visit her, someone she hadn't seen in quite a while and the preparations for his visit were draining her somewhat.

Jeff Gutterman

"I don't understand. You once told me that energy couldn't be reduced. That there was an unending stream of it for all of us."

"You're right, Cashel, in all but one way. If you remember, what I told you was that energy can never be extinguished. It exists always and always will. But there are times when it can be reduced."

"How do you reduce it?"

"By giving your power away. And before you ask, the answer is by allowing others to influence you beyond what you feel is correct for you."

"But you're too strong to do that."

"I'd like to think so, but the Hollows are getting part of what they want."

"I don't understand."

Tandara looked long and hard at Cashel, hesitated and then smiled. "In a way, I have a very special bond with one of them."

Cashel's mouth dropped open and a small gasp escaped her lips. "You know one of them?"

"Yes. And I agreed a long time ago to keep the communication system between us open. Always, no matter what. So you see, I've opened myself to someone else's influence."

"Can't you break that agreement."

"Once given, I never go back on my word Cashel. That's the integrity of who I am. That's

what makes me unique to myself and others."
Cashel could only smile. But it was a disturbed
smile and Tandara was quick to pick it up.
"Cashel, in time you'll learn that there's more to
you then you can imagine. There's the good and
wonderful part of you that you know. And there's
a shadow side of yourself that seeps through
every now and then. You can't disown it because
it's you. So, to the best of your ability you inte-
grate it, by accommodating and harmonizing
with it the best you can. That's the only thing that
will keep you balanced. If you refuse to
acknowledge it, then it works within you creating
disharmony."

"I think I understand. Kind of like what you
said about Goble working with his past."

"Yes, in a way."

"Will you ever be friends with this Hollow
again?"

"The one who leads them has convinced them
all, including the one I have a special bond with,
that it was me who forced them to inhabit space
the way they now exist, as soulless spirits.
Unfortunately, they've all chosen to believe him,
taking no responsibility for themselves and what
they've created whatsoever. That's caused a lot of
bad feelings to be targeted toward me. As much
as I dislike that, I can accept what's happened and

forgive those who innocently believed something that wasn't true. So, to answer your question. On my side, I'm open. On their side, well, it's completely up to them. It's something that's out of my hands."

"How did the Hollows become soulless?"

Tandara was quiet, glancing over at the beauty that was Cashel. "Did you know that before you came here you were in a very large unmarked space, viewing physical life through a big picture window. You, like many others, wondered what it would be like to enter physical reality and experience it. You wanted to touch something and feel its essence. You wanted to feel something and know its individual soul. That part of All That Is that is attached to the entire universe."

Cashel had heard part of this once before when the two had shared some quiet moments alone, but even now was mesmerized by Tandara's voice, and wasn't about to move an eyelash, thinking she would miss something that Tandara hadn't uncovered in the past.

"You were given what you needed and allowed to enter. You were given a soul. A soul that exists because of its very connection to All That Is. A soul that is enhanced by the emotion of love because of its connection to All That Is. A soul that is pure energy, pure light, pure love. A soul that mixes with the physical shell to sustain physical life as we know it. All that you know, for we've talked of that before. But did you know that for the soul to remain with the physical shell, for it to continue to exist at all, it must express and enhance the love that is a part of its very nature. If it's unable to do that, for whatever reason, it must follow the rules set down by the universe, by All That Is, and withdraw from the physical shell. That will in turn, in a very short time, cause the physical shell to wither and die."

Cashel was unable to generate an independent thought as wrapped up as she was in Tandara's gift of knowledge. At best, when a fleeting impression left its image on her mind's eye, it moved at a pace much too fast to corral and interpret. Involuntarily her mouth began forming the words of the impression, obvious to Tandara that she lacked the additional energy necessary to bring her lips together for vocal expression.

"You asked how the Hollows became soulless."

Barely perceptible was an acknowledged nod from Cashel, but that was as far as her endorsement of Tandara's question would take her.

"For those souls that freely chose to blend with the physical universe by taking on a physical shell, the law required that the energy of positive emotion was to be passed on and multiplied as love. And, in one way or another, most people chose to do just that. But there were those who chose instead to pass on their negative emotions through anger and deceit, continually influencing and helping to rob others of their own power. It was at this point that All That Is chose to take back the positive emotion that existed within each of those spirits. Because each soul needs positive emotion to sustain it, they lost their souls. Within each of their spirits they became empty, no positive emotions existing within them. Over time they became known as the Hollows, never allowed to fully take on any particular form, no matter what dimension they chose to experience. They would only be allowed to exist within the void that existed within them."

Goble and Dragit had shared many long conversations over the six day period, Dragit surprisingly seeking additional knowledge, but keeping somewhat to form, constantly questioning any presented to him.

Before the sixth night had completed itself, Goble could feel Dragit's question moving around inside him much like a pebble having just been launched into a quiet stream.

"You're not going to answer me are you?"

"Dragit I'm not sure how to answer you. More than that, I'm concerned that you'd even ask a question like that."

Dragit looked straight at Goble and shook his head as if the reversal had happened. He was the teacher and Goble the student. "Okay, okay. Boy, you're as bad as Cashel. Forget I asked you about you. I don't want to know what happens when you die. Tell me what happens when one of the Hollows dies instead?"

"Dragit, as you understand death, they're already dead."

"How can they be dead if they're here?"

"Oh boy . . . Let me try answering your first question. When I die, my consciousness will automatically flow into the greater part of itself, which thankfully, is an energy pattern that is very positive and loving."

"And if it wasn't."

"Then it would be negative and fearful, and I'd attract that kind of energy when I died."

"Would you always have that kind of energy around you?"

"Hopefully not. I'd try and remember everything that I had learned in the past. And, if I listened real well, somewhere deep inside me a voice would whisper, slowly and clearly, that I create my own reality, and if I didn't like the situation I was in, all I'd have to do would be to change my thought pattern and attract a different kind of energy."

"Oh. That's pretty simple. What else can you tell me?"

"I predict that as you close those heavy eyelids sleep will come quickly for you."

"You just don't want to talk anymore."

"Dragit I can't imagine where you got that idea. Close your eyes and sleep, sleep, sleep . . ."

They all heard it at the same time. A loud piercing cry, an echo within itself, as if coming from the belly of a whale. Both Cashel and Dragit, separated by the distance between rooms, shot straight up at the same time. Neither moved a muscle nor twitched a hair. They were momentary granite, frozen in position.

Tandara and Goble reacted a little differently, each throwing off their bed covers and heading for the sound, somewhere in the house. Tandara moved through the door closest to her first,

The Passage, the Gift, and the Prophecy

coming to an immediate stop less than several feet into the kitchen when the sound began again. Visually spanning the length of the room and seeing nothing out of place, she made it to the next door and passed into the living room area. Moving quickly from one side of the room to the other she noticed nothing out of place here either.

Goble, leaving the meditation room through the only door available to him, moved quickly around the perimeter of the hallway, choosing not to enter either the dimensional room he had been introduced to by Tandara or the third companion room off the hallway that he knew nothing about. When he found the hallway clear he made his way toward the library. What he saw shook him to the bone.

Tandara had apparently moved much quicker than he had toward the sound. When he entered the room he found her behind one of the chairs staring up at a most formidable figure. Its foundation was the center of the coffee table, with a spread that covered every inch of its glass top. Moving its bulk at a slow pace toward the ceiling it had taken on the form of a man. An old sea captain.

By the time Cashel and Dragit had snapped out of their stupor, Tandara and Goble had already entered the library. Cashel was the first to leave the warmth of her bed to bravely go in search of Tandara. Walking slowly at first, not quite sure what was around each corner, she tip-toed lightly over the wooden floor, following the path she believed Tandara had taken moments before. Passing first through the bedroom door to the kitchen, she suspended her movement as Tandara had done, and peered at all the non-moving objects on the walls and sink. Only when she was satisfied that nothing in the kitchen had emitted the piercing, high-pitched wail they had heard, or was now holding Tandara prisoner, did she move on to the living room area.

Now in the living room, she once again brought her body to a state of rigid attention, those large wonderful eyes of hers responding to every speck of dust that floated bewitchingly through the air. She watched as the particles of matter moved in random directions, this way and that, never really seeming to land anywhere, as though perpetually riding on an invisible magic carpet.

Softly and slowly she moved her lips apart, and with an involuntary upward motion, her tongue touched the roof of her mouth and called her mentors name. "Tandara, this is Cashel. Can you hear me? Where are you? Tandara? . . ."

There was no response, which only worked to intensify the feeling of a growing uneasiness within her. She could feel the heat rising up the small of her back and knew that the tiny hair at the nape of her neck standing was at attention. Her call was becoming a whisper. "Tandara? . . ."

Continuing her tiptoe-like motion forward, she moved at a snail's pace toward the other end of the living room, all her senses at their peak. Now within several feet of the door to the library, about to take the final step that would put her within its chamber, she heard it again and froze. But this time the loud uncomfortable sound had company. Coming from somewhere within the alcove of the room she was about to enter, what she couldn't as yet see, were a host of powerful, noisy, electrical sparks. Each one moved through the air in a random direction, for a split second lighting up only its own shaft and then immediately burning itself out, not just disappearing, but leaving a black streak across the invisible atmosphere of the room that it had just crossed.

With her heart pounding loud enough that she thought it could be heard by anyone within the house, she forced herself to attempt another step toward the unknown. Without warning, out of nowhere, heading toward her at a disoriented run, came Dragit. Trying in vain to either slow

Jeff Gutterman

down or get his feet to move him in the direction he wanted them to, he spotted his sister too late. "Cashel, look out!" Ramming her like the caboose of a train and attaching itself to the other cars before the engine moved them forward, Dragit grabbed her from behind, scaring the daylights out of her. With an unstoppable momentum, he began moving them both toward the interior of the library. Advancing quickly, they had almost moved the seven paces necessary to reach the center of the room. But before that happened, the perpetual motion machine now sliding across the floor caught their feet on the ends of the Indian throw rug, and caused it to bunch together and make their attempt at stopping any further progression, one of fantasy.

They needn't of worried. Using one of the chairs as a stopping block, they both flipped over and landed on its cushion, now in such a position that they ended up staring straight into the face of some huge figure in the center of the coffee table. Neither of them were aware of either Tandara or Goble, both of them feet away from each other.

"Dragit, will you let go of me! Something's poking me in the back." As Dragit moved from under her to her side, she reached behind her back and produced one of the ancient books that had been floating above the cushion before she had flipped over and landed on it. She let go of the book as quickly as she had retrieved it. "That hurts. It's like a piece of ice."

It was Dragit's turn. "Let me see."

He froze when he heard Goble's voice. "Don't touch that!"

Both of them, frightened by the tone in Goble's voice, turned and gazed at both their friends. Noticing that neither Tandara nor Goble was making any attempt at moving toward them, they both tried to get up and move toward them. The thought and attempted action were in vain. Neither could move. Frightened, they both turned their attention toward the figure directly in front of them.

In a very soft moving motion the sea captain reached down to take Cashel's hand. Without saying a word she reached up toward the Hollows energy, extending her hand toward him as he had done toward her.

The voice was once again Goble's. "Cashel, no. Withdraw your hand!"

"I can't. It just seems to be moving by itself."

Inches apart, continuing to move in slow motion, Cashel was beginning to understand that the touch of this sea captain was something she didn't want. And she began to tear. Dragit, eyes riveted and bouncing back and forth between the two adults and whatever was floating in front of him, still found the energy to move further and further into the softness of the chair he was sharing with Cashel.

"Tandara, please . . . help me. Please!"

"Focus on the tenets Cashel, the tenets," demanded Goble.

Even though she was unable to stop her hand from moving out to connect with the figures, Goble's demand broke her spell. She moved her eyes only once more toward Tandara, not understanding why she wasn't saying or doing anything to help, and then focused her attention on the tenets on the old manuscript. Immediately, the fourth tenet flashed before her inner picture screen. She reviewed the entire tenet, took a deep breath and began her mental withdrawal, rearranging and then constantly repeating to herself the essence of the words of the tenet. "I have my own power. It's not something I choose to give away. My thoughts and the motions of my body are mine and under my control."

Before their touch was complete Cashel was able to begin to retract her hand back toward her side. The sparks flew in every direction possible, causing the books scattered around the library to take wing and fly in disoriented directions throughout the room, at times individually targeting all four of them before returning hap-hazardly to their confused directions.

The sparks broke Dragit's spell. "I've never seen anything like this before. Who is he?"

Goble looked toward the Hollow and then at Dragit. "His name is Magus. He's the leader of the Hollows."

"But he looks like a pirate or something. That eye patch and those teeth. And that dirty beard, ugh."

"Pirate indeed. He'll steal what he can. Remember your lessons well Dragit, remember them well."

"Can't he talk?"

"Not in the way you understand."

Cashel had regained some of her power back and was beginning to feel it. "What's wrong with Tandara? Why won't she talk to me? Did I do something wrong?"

"You did nothing wrong, Cashel. Tandara needs to focus her attention and energy on Magus to keep him from moving anywhere else within the house, and to keep us all from harm. Somehow, he entered this house when he wasn't supposed to. The energy field on the outside perimeter of the plateau was supposed to keep them all out."

"But how did he get by the energy shields?"

"I'm not sure. My guess is that he violated some of his own Hollows to do it."

"But how?"

"Probably by either tricking or forcing them to move against the shield at just the right moment. It's possible that when their energy exploded and dispersed they would have been able to move through the shield freely. I suppose if it were timed right it would work. And once inside the perimeter he probably used a similar technique to pass the energy of the candles and enter the library. It was his energy that Tandara sensed in the room. His energy that was making the ancient books float in space. And more than likely his doing, that one of the ancient books is missing."

Dragit was now up from the chair moving around the formed energy coming from the center of the coffee table. "He sure is ugly, isn't he? What happened to his feet?"

"Nothing happened to his feet Dragit. He never had any. He's simply taken on a form that he thought would be frightening to us."

"I'm not afraid of him, dirty old hair and all."

"I'm afraid the bigger question is how was he able to take on form at all? That's probably something Tandara's trying to understand now. There just might be a rebel among the Hollows."

"A rebel? What's that mean?"

Goble had Cashel's full attention now. Her beloved horse Palimar kept flashing before her eyes. Was that what Goble had meant? "Goble, is Palimar coming back?"

"No, actually that's not quite what I mean by a rebel, Cashel." Goble closed his physical eyes and concentrated with all his might, trying to remember back when. Information was returning to him at a very slow pace and it was frustrating him. When he opened his eyes he was looking right at Cashel. "What I think has happened is that one of the Hollows wants to cross over, not be a Hollow anymore."

"Can they do that?"

"Under certain circumstances, yes. But it takes a Hollow a long time to get to that point and once the decision is made and a door is opened, it opens it for all of the Hollows at once. Most of them would never know about it. But Magus is pretty smart. He controls the Hollows so closely that without them being aware of it he shares many of their thoughts when he chooses. I'm just guessing, but I think that's what's happened."

"Who is the Hollow that's trying to leave?"

"I haven't a clue, but if I'm right we'll have another visitor shortly."

Cashel was lost in thought. "Goble, can't Magus hear us?"

"No. That's why we can talk freely around him. Nor does he see physical reality the way we do. He senses energy. That's why both Tandara and I have been after the two of you to center yourself."

Cashel was out of her chair and through the library door that led to Tandara's bedroom before either of them could stop her. She returned a moment later with her manuscript, *Gifts of Perception*. "I've still got two more tenets to read."

Before he could respond he noticed that something was causing Tandara's focus to slip. She glanced toward Goble. "Can you hear that?"

Cocking his head to one side, Goble listened intently before responding. No, nothing really."

"I'm sure I heard him."

"Heard who, Tandara?"

"The Toucan."

Tandara's momentary loss of focus was all Magus needed to sense. With the swoop of his large electrical hand he reached down for her, wrapping his illusionary palm around her entire physical structure. With little effort he simply scooped her up, noticeably ending not only her physical presence in the room they were all sharing, but his as well. With Magus' departure, the energy that the library had been exposed to immediately dissipated, and the ancient books that had been floating above the chairs collapsed on their respective cushions.

Cashel was heartbroken. She had now lost her two closest friends and it seemed as though there was nothing she could do about it. Her brother on the other hand was angry. He wanted to do something to help but had no idea what or how. And Goble was frustrated beyond what he felt his normal limits to be. Glancing from one to the other he tried his best to comfort them, knowing full well that he needed comfort himself. He had to do something. Anything was better than no movement at all.

"If you'll both wait for me here, I'll be back shortly. There's something that needs attending to." With that, Goble headed toward the door to the library.

"Wait," cried Dragit. "You said we might have another visitor."

"It may very well happen. I should be back before that, but it doesn't matter if I'm not. Whoever comes will not be one to fear." Now, almost through the doorway, Goble turned back toward them. "If anything, they'll need your help."

Dragit wasn't completely satisfied with Goble's answer. "How will we know if the person that shows up is actually who they say they are?"

"It's simple, Dragit. Ask your heart. The correct answer will always come from there."

Dragit began pacing again, using all of his newfound knowledge to think of a way to get Tandara back. Cashel took a different route, opening the manuscript to the tenth tenet she began to read.

THE TENTH TENET

Sense what's in your heart as the truth. Everything else is an illusion"

Intellect is a wonderful part of your physical experience, but should never guide you into something if your inner feelings are to move you away from it. Trust only what you sense deep down inside yourself, for your chosen path is filled with many illusionary perceptions. Growth comes about by moving

through these deceptions and around the imaginary
barriers you've allowed them to create.

"Dragit, Tandara and Palimar are both okay.
And somehow they're going to come back. I just
know it."

"Maybe, maybe not."

"You just don't know how powerful they are.
How much they each believe in themselves.
They're fine and they're coming back, you'll see."

"I think they need help."

"I didn't say they didn't need help." Cashel
grabbed Dragit by the hand. "Come on."

"Where are we going? Goble told us to stay
here."

"I know he did, but he didn't tell us who we
were going to meet if someone did come. Just
how to tell if they were friendly. If that happens
then everything's okay. But if we're going to meet
another Hollow, a friendly one if there is such a
thing, we have to do it outside. They won't be
able to get any further than the energy shields the
way Magus did, if we get it wrong."

Dragit thought a moment, gave a wise old
man's nod, and allowed Cashel to lead him out of

the library to the front door and the fresh air on the outside.

———————————————

As Goble left the library he circled the inner hallway, stopping in front of the one door he had never passed through before. What awaited him was the unknown. Reaching for the doorknob he hesitated, unsure whether or not to enter. In seconds he made his decision. "Tandara, forgive me for entering what you once told me was your sanctuary. But with all that's happened, I feel that something in this room will help you and in turn help us all.

With the mixed feelings of love and resignation, knowing he was entering a very private arena, he moved his hand on the doorknob in a rotating motion and pushed open the door. Initially confused he reached for the second door and repeated the exercise. And then the third and the fourth, each succeeding door becoming larger and harder to move through. On the other side of the fourth door was another circular hallway that would allow him to move in either direction to a position one hundred and eighty degrees from the point he

The Passage, the Gift, and the Prophecy

stood at. He was now facing three more doors and knew instinctively that only one of the doors would be open to him.

Looking from door to door, unable to make a choice for fear that it would be the wrong one, he thought he heard a small voice off to one side of the hallway. It was Tandara's. "Focus Goble, focus. See the love in everything and everyone. Whatever door you choose with that vision will be the correct one."

Lightheaded and suddenly weak, he closed his eyes and smiled, imagining Tandara, Cashel, and Dragit along with him and the intensity of who they were in spirit. Then he thought of Palimar and Ginruss and how full of the life-giving spirit they each were. He opened his eyes. But it was not complete and he knew it. Once again he allowed his lids to droop and the wave of energy move through him as he thought of Magus and the other Hollows. It was harder. It took longer. But slowly the image of their true spirits emerged before his vision. As with every living thing, they were at the core of their being, love. His recognition caused his eyes to open suddenly and eventually a smile to cross his face.

He reached for the middle door and turned the knob.

Magus had given Palimar little choice. When Palimar had dispersed his scout so easily from the mountaintop he knew he would be confronted with another force at least equal to Tandara's. That had frightened him. Two Tandara's was more then he could handle and he didn't want to fail as he had the last time. Even if the Toucan didn't show up this time he was unsure of the extent of Palimar's powers and hadn't wanted to take a chance.

He had needed something that would work for him and bring Palimar over to his side. But what could it be? That ancient horse had everything he wanted. He could change shape or color and travel to different realities and dimensions. He had the ability to talk if he chose. Or make himself physical at will. He gathered friends by the energy he created around himself and had the respect of those that he gathered. Frustration, anxiety, oh, the burdens of leadership.

With a thunderous rage, the old Sea Captain had thrown a series of powerful thunderbolts at the other Hollows, dispersing many of them to the corners of the universe.

"Magus, you need to calm down." Celone had happily been one of those he had missed. But of course, he thought. That was it. Celone was the key. He would use her to get to Palimar. She was getting weak anyway. He had read her thoughts many times before without her knowing it. He knew that at the first reasonable chance she would attempt to cross over. He also knew that she would get help from Tandara when that moment finally came. And at that point, Tandara would ask for Palimar's help. There was enough power between them to return her soul to her. So he thought.

Years ago, Magus had given Celone an appropriate position within the Hollows so that he could keep his eye on her. He had always suspected an agreement with Tandara of one type or another. Even if she had denied it.

"Magus, you're wrong. There's no such agreement. I hate my sister more than you know."

"But you didn't always hate her."

"She was the cause of all of my problems. I tell you I hate her and would make no agreement with her."

His voice boomed throughout the space they occupied and Celone realized that for the first time she was frightened of Magus. The bellow that was his voice was strong and narrowly focused. "I don't believe you!"

Magus had not gained his power from being overly stupid. Some of his delusions were well thought out. This one also fit quite well with his thought process. He reasoned that if Celone had a secret pact with Tandara, then Palimar must also have a secret pack with her to help Celone if she ever chose to cross over. And because of who he was, he would always put others before himself. He needed to convince Palimar that Celone was at the point of crossing over and that he was aware of it. Unless Palimar agreed to join them, he would aggravate Celone's efforts by diminishing and dispersing her spirit to such a great degree, that the same spirit would never operate as one whole body again. Knowing the connection between Tandara and Celone, Palimar would have to give in. He had thought it a masterful plan. And it had worked. Palimar was now one of them.

The plateau looked funny, split somewhat down the middle. Both Cashel and Dragit walked to the edge of the crack and peered down into its depths.

Acting as the intellectual, Dragit spoke first. "They must be very powerful to have done this."

"Dragit, look! Up there. What do you think it is?"

His forehead furrowed and his young facial lines showed themselves as he glanced to that area of the sky that Cashel was pointing to.

Flying about fifty feet above them in a circular pattern was the strangest bird they had ever laid eyes on. And the most beautiful. Only two feet in length he forced their upward focus.

"Dragit, look at how beautiful he is. He's all different colors."

"He's got the largest nose I've ever seen."

"That's his mouth."

"Nose, mouth. It doesn't matter. It's still the biggest thing I've ever seen. What do you suppose he is?"

The Toucan descended several times to within a few feet of them, slowing himself just enough so that they would be able to get a good look at him and then again retracting and allowing the wind current to carry him around the plateau.

"I've never seen so many colors on one bird before. He's yellow and blue and green and white."

"And black and orange and brown. Dragit I've got it . . . This is the Toucan Tandara was talking about."

"How do you know that?"

"I don't know, I just do. How else could he have gotten through the energy shields?"

Dragit was quick to respond. "Don't ask silly questions. He's magical like Tandara. Maybe he's here to help us."

"Look! We've got another visitor," was all she could think to say, as the energy apparition that looked like Tandara began forming before them.

Chapter Nine

As he closed the door behind him he thought his vision had begun to blur. Most of the room was shrouded in a white mist of some sort. He moved through it slowly, unsure of what was located in the immediate space before him. Without understanding just how, he had walked in a circle around the room, recognizing that with each step, he was moving in an upward spiral without the feeling of having done so. Within seconds he found himself facing a whitish blue pulsating structure whose expression was that of a circular staircase.

With an obvious commanding gait, he began the gentle climb to the top, being only slightly aware that with each step forward he was moving deeper within himself. Looking up, he realized that the circular structure's height was well beyond where a normal ceiling should have been. At the top, Goble stopped and gazed in awe. "What in the world?"

Before him lay a small suspension bridge, no more than several feet wide, running a distance well into the unknown. As he stepped onto the bridge and looked over, it became apparent that the overpass had come equipped with an ocean of water below it.

Goble's mind began to freeze. Not being able to see the end of the bridge he wasn't sure he should begin the excursion across it. But he also understood that retreating back down the staircase would not allow him the results he wanted. So his journey began.

———————————

On the plateau, the apparition before them was becoming smaller and more dense. Cashel was leaning into it, Dragit not able to see a thing. At first glance she was sure it was Tandara, but the next retreated to uncertainty.

Cashel was beside herself. "I don't understand. It looks like her, but it doesn't look like her. I think the Hollows forced her to be one of them." Then, throwing her arms somewhat up into the air in frustration she offered an explanation to Dragit. "Maybe that's why Goble said we'd have nothing to fear from the next Hollow."

"I don't know what you're talking about. I can't see anything but the bird."

"Dragit, you must be able to see her. She's right in front of you. Even the Toucan is flying around her."

"I don't know what he's flying around, but I don't see anything."

The Toucan was indeed flying around the image appearing to Cashel. It was Celone. He had been called upon to protect her. It was necessary, as she was making preparations for her transition, that she be allowed to do it without interference. Arrangements had been made long ago with Tandara that when Celone was ready to make the cross over and begin to reclaim her soul, the Toucan would help in the way that he could. Because of his friendship with Tandara he would help her sister begin to return to the world of All That Is. It was up to Celone. But mostly it was up to the Toucan. Even Tandara didn't possess the power and direct linkage to All That Is that he did.

Cashel was moving further into the newly changing apparition, recalling Goble's ever-present words that there would be nothing to fear from the next Hollow that chose to visit. "I think she's trying to speak. She's trying to say something."

Finding it harder and harder to focus on the appearance before her, and unable to understand just what she was saying, Cashel was once again becoming frustrated. But it mattered little. With one very quick circular motion, the Toucan wrapped a very thin line of brilliant, fire-like string around Celone and within seconds she was gone, leaving him circling in the space she had just occupied.

Palimar was waiting for just the right moment. He knew what Tandara was up to and she him, but they had been unable to tell the others. Together, they were the only two strong enough at this point to block their thoughts from reaching and being shared by Magus or the other Hollows.

Allowing the Hollows to think that he had crossed over for the very reasons Magus had outlined in his mind, Palimar, in the cold black void that housed the Hollows, had been sending them waves of energy, working to lighten their normal negative vibratory force. It had worked. The mixed energy unbalanced their own and temporarily caused them to have doubts about what they were doing. Even Magus, as strong as he was, wavered at times.

But most importantly, the intermittent frequency of positive energy that Palimar had been sending, worked its magic on Celone, giving her that last minute boost that she needed, bringing her closer to her new goal at a much faster pace. Tandara and Celone were now talking.

Goble stopped on the only walkway on the expansion bridge and looked down. It was a long way to the bottom, but unlike the magical old wooden well on the plateau, he could see the surface of the water. A quiet surreal sea, dark blue and crystal clear. As he peered into it, even as far away as he knew he was, he began to see a

Jeff Gutterman

reflection of himself glancing back, quietly offering him something. A book. An old book. An old ancient book.

Unable to contain his excitement at his new find, he shouted to no one in particular, "It's the missing fourth book." His own image, many times his own size, was offering its return. Instinctively he reached down toward the image, hoping to receive the gift from himself. His action was in vain. The image was not handing him the book but rather opening it for him to look into. It was very confusing. All he was able to make out on the page of the book that had been opened to him was the fact that it was outlined in a dynamic golden white light. Other than that, the page appeared blank.

A few moments after the open book had been offered, it began to dissolve into a billion microscopic atoms, each bumping into the other and dispersing into the universe. Goble had no choice but to continue his journey toward the end of the bridge. He immediately became aware that with each step, he was moving into an atmosphere of lightness as though losing his physical presence. It was somewhat the same feeling he had in Tandara's other dimensional room, when he was reviewing his past and learning to center himself by reexperiencing and balancing all of his previous past selves. But this time he wasn't having to spin and rotate his physical body to generate the physical breakdown, to disengage the atomic glue that held it together. Here it was automatically disintegrating, freeing him from the physical dimension.

He found himself in an alien world, unlike any he had experienced before. Other spirits floated by him, some offering acknowledgment, some not, but all friendly. In this reality if he saw a distant star and wondered at its world, it would instantly come to him, its energy arms wide, offering all of itself.

He walked on, not really walking at all, his now imaginary heart very light, having accomplished a distant goal. It was a game he thought and there are different ways to move the pieces forward, each moving only if the other pieces were already within their protective boundaries. He was feeling wonderful. So much so in fact that he almost forgot why he had entered Tandara's sanctuary to begin with. But sooner than not, the memory returned, and along with it the furrowed lines of concern on his forehead. Tandara was in trouble and he needed to do everything he could to help her.

"My eyes keep searching for something and seeing nothing. Yet I know that somewhere within this sanctuary is the answer I seek to help my very dear friend. Look in every opening of the mist Goble, every opening. Somewhere is the answer I seek."

The thought occurred to him that one of the spirits floating by may be able to help. But as he turned to catch the next one's nonphysical glance they had all disappeared. "I'm on my own. Okay. Focus Goble, focus. I still can't see the end of the bridge, yet I know I'm very close to what I'm looking for. It's here. The answer's here, somewhere within that old ancient book."

Dragit hadn't been able to see Celone but something inside him believed Cashel when she said she had seen something. Maybe it was the fact that he couldn't see Palimar either but believed he existed. Or maybe it was something deep down inside him that gave him that all-confident knowing that only comes from within. Whatever the reason, he understood that he and he alone, could get Tandara back.

Cashel on the other hand was losing herself in Ginruss, together the two of them moving from one side of the plateau to the breach down the middle, veering over, looking for Hollows.

"I think they look like pirates, Ginruss. Big, straggly hair with dirty beards and an eye patch over one eye. Oh yeah, two wooden legs. But they're big. Real big. Not very good looking, Ginruss. Not very good looking at all."

Dragit had walked to the corner of the plateau, close to the shield behind the house. There he sat down, closed his eyes and concentrated. He tried with all his might to bring a picture of her face into his vision. And then slowly he had it. What he saw on the screen before his mind's eye startled him. It was Tandara. And not just her face had come into his field of vision but her entire physical presence. She was bound with something, unable to move any part of her body whatsoever. It looked like she was trying to move, call out in some way. "Uh oh. Tandara, I know I can help you. Just tell me how to get to you."

Tandara and Celone had talked for a long time, each trying to understand the other. Tandara had made a great deal of progress in her discussions, convincing Celone that it wasn't her that had taken her soul. That she didn't exercise that kind of power. She believed Celone now understood.

Celone had been the first to speak. "I've hated you for a long time."

"I've never hated you. But to the degree that I could, I did distance myself from that part of you that hated a part of yourself. It's hard for all of us at times to look deep down within our being and bring up thoughts and ideas that don't fit comfortably within us. It's much easier to blame something or someone outside ourselves."

"You never supported my efforts when I was physical."

"A good portion of the efforts you were involved in were not those that I could support. They affected others in a negative way. That's not who I was. Who I am. As for the idea of not supporting you at all, you have always had it within yourself to provide whatever measure of support you needed without looking for approval from the outside. And you've always known that."

These were the last few minutes of their conversation and it was apparent that Celone was breaking down, moving away from her hardened stance and accepting Tandara's comments, allowing a different perception within her to build.

"My soul. Can you help me get it back? Where I exist is not life of any nature that is known. It is black and empty, disheartening and cold."

"Celone, if you choose to return, you do so without the answer you seek. As I've told you, I wasn't the one that removed your soul from you, so I'm not in a position to give it back to you. But to have made the effort you have in contacting me and wanting to talk, you've taken a giant step in the right direction. And because of that I've asked an old friend who has great influence with All That Is to help you. He's doing what he can."

"When you allowed me to pass through the energy that guarded the plateau I did feel someone else's energy. I haven't felt that for a very long time."

Tandara smiled across at her sister. "Yes. That would be my friend the Toucan. He's waiting for you to make a final decision."

Cashel was sitting with Ginruss, silently reviewing the first ten tenets. According to some very forbidding instructions on the page after the tenth tenet, she was not allowed to turn the page to read the final one until the previous ten were known and understood. Once her review was complete, feeling fairly confident that she knew and understood each doctrine, she turned the page of instructions to gaze on the last principle of Tandara's manuscript. More than disappointment showed on her face.

"Oh Ginruss look. Someone has torn the final tenet out of the manuscript. Why would they do that . . . It must be very important."

As for Goble, he was still suspended somewhere between time and space in the sanctuary, without his physical body, on a bridge in another dimension. He chose to continue moving forward feeling certain that he was doing the right thing. He was soon rewarded.

Less than a few feet in front of him, drifting within the expanse of this very unique dimension was a simple book, ancient in detail. "There you are." Goble moved his hand out to meet the compressed atomic vibration, missing it, not having reached far enough, and then pulling his now nonphysical hand back to himself without it. It didn't matter. The physical grasp was unnecessary. Just the return movement of his hand along with a thought of what he wanted, automatically moved the missing ancient book toward him.

Opening it he discovered all of the pages blank save one. What he saw took him back minutes

The Passage, the Gift, and the Prophecy

before to the vision in the crystal water below. In the center of the book on a sheet of physical paper, one side of its edges appearing fragmented and torn, all of its surrounding edges laced in brilliant golden white light, was Cashel's missing final tenet, a tenet not even Goble had seen before.

Dragit was still sitting behind the house when he began getting lightheaded and thought he was seeing things. With his eyes wide open he realized that just outside the perimeter of the rope-like light, he was gazing at hundreds of energy forms. The Hollows had made it to the top of the plateau.

"Oh boy. Goble! Where are you Goble. We've got a bit of a problem here. Goble . . ." His voice was trailing off, his vision blurring or so he thought. Now, along with the Hollows, he saw a large electrical horse standing beside two separate images of Tandara. Now he was real concerned, trying to remove himself from his physical position but unable to garner the strength to do so. So he began drifting. Drifting . . .

All of a sudden Cashel's thoughts were also drifting. But they were more defined. They were only on Goble. And Goble's thoughts were on the ancient page of the manuscript before him. The final tenet.

THE FINAL TENET

Life. Physical. Nonphysical. Is a game. The only reality
behind it is that of Thought, Creation, and Movement.
Life is about changes. Nothing stays the same.

All that you see before you doesn't really exist,
except in your mind where all things are possible.
Pull toward you the visions you wish to experience
and reject those that you do not. If you are wholly
yourself, you can only magnetize those things to you
that are truth and thereafter positive experiences.
Anything else entering the world of your mind, means
you are not being who you really are in all
circumstances, and therefore by your own initiation,
you hold back the light of love from your true being.
Strive always to be uplifting and positive.
Strive always to be you.

They were connected, all of them. As he read,
Goble moved the image of the final tenet along to
both Cashel and Dragit. Understanding what she

was being given, she now moved with Ginruss to the back of the house by the large invisible shield. Although the invisibility maintained itself, the shield continued to both accept and repel its own light source, a point of fiery-like rope from the other two shields on the plateau. Below it she found the lone figure of her younger brother sitting on the grass. With a feeling of pride welling up inside her, she watched in awe as Dragit became who he was and began his dialogue with the Hollows.

Epilogue

"I know I'm just a child, but you need to listen to me. You all believe you have to be who you've been told you are. That's not true. You can be anything and anyone you want. The only thing that's holding you where you are is your belief that you belong there. You're all free to go your own way without looking to a leader for blessings to do so. You don't have to dishonor others. Everyone can have what they want. There's enough energy there for all of you. All you have to do is want it. You're holding some friends of mine. They're friends to you also, if you'll allow them to be. You've been blaming them for something they didn't do. They don't have the power to take

Jeff Gutterman

your soul. Only All That Is has that power, and deep down you all know that. It can be returned to you if you allow it. Now grow up, take responsibility for yourselves and release my friends!"

As the individual Hollows began to take in Dragit's words and watched as Celone freely moved with Tandara into a physical presence, Magus began to receive much of the negative vibration they had been harboring for him. It was more than he could stand. With a mighty explosion that moved the giant mountain back and forth, he distributed himself in many millions of pieces to the far corners of the universe. With the release of the illusionary hold Magus had on them, they began to descend Tandara's mountain with thoughts of a new beginning.

Cashel, looking up at Tandara and Celone, understood by Tandara's smile that she had never really been a captive of Magus and the Hollows. Nor had Palimar changed sides. She felt ashamed of herself at having believed so little in Palimar's heart and foolish at doubting Tandara's powers.

"There's no reason to feel that way. Goble also fell into that trap. Perception can be stronger than truth only if you allow it to. In this case, all of your perceptions eventually allowed you to grow. That was part of the necessity of my pretense in not knowing what had happened to Palimar. I won't apologize for it, for it served its purpose well. Each of you chose a different passage to get here, a different perception. Each of those perceptions allowed you only what you allowed it to, all the time forgetting who you really were and how much power you really have to maintain a positive focus all the time. Here on the mountaintop over the last seven days your brother found more of who he really is. He found his strength and in so doing will begin to view aspects of his life a little differently now. Goble discovered that by acknowledging a lost part of himself he became whole, and that alone allowed him to accept his greater power and showed him that he can really do whatever he wanted to. And you, dear one, have found more of the knowledge you sought to be the teacher you truly are."

"We owe you so much."

"Not at all. I owe you. All of you helped with the Hollows. Without your wonderful strength my sister may not have been able to return from them."

"Your sister?"

"Her identical sister, Celone." It was Goble's voice as he walked toward them. And a very old friend of mine."

Goble crocked his head ever so slightly to the right. "They never breached the library did they?"

"No. The energy surrounding the plateau can never be breached."

Dragit's eyes were wide as she pointed up, now seeing what he hadn't been able to before. "He breached it."

The Toucan circled all of them three times, passing closest to Tandara, then moved many feet above them and began circling the plateau once again. On his first pass, the entire mountain began to shake and move as the two halves of the plateau began to come together and reassemble themselves into one whole. On his second pass the two halves sealed themselves to each other, and the rope-like pulsating light that had been bouncing from one shield to the next, began to diminish its brilliance until it became still once again. On his third and final pass he dipped his wings to say goodbye to his friends before adjusting his thought and moving inconspicuously into another dimension.

Standing on the mountaintop watching Palimar return to them, Tandara, Goble, Cashel, Ginruss, Celone, and even Dragit, who had now changed his perception enough to see him, really understood how lucky they were to have Palimar as their friend.

Becoming more physical with each moment and now within an arms reach of them, stood a loving and wise golden chestnut horse with a white mane and tail. In a voice all could hear he had the following to say: "Before the Toucan left he asked me to relay something for him to you all. Something he felt would be helpful to those you continue to come into contact with. In a way, his words will foreshadow the future for all of us. What he had to say was simply this . . . 'If the incidence of the Hollows had occurred in the village below, the village would have suffered greatly. The people, no matter what their status or power, live within a perceptual lack and from that lack project the emotion of fear into their lives. In the future, as the valley people continue their individual journeys, there will be many new and sometimes unpleasant trials, some unheard and unthought of, some previously discussed and passed over to each succeeding generation. These trials and circumstances are an opportunity for enhanced growth, because of the speed at which they will come to them. It's up to all of you, each in your own way, to help change the perceptions of lack and blame into abundance and acceptance. Only by making others understand that their thoughts create their reality can this be done. Only by allowing people the opportunity to accept responsibility for who and how powerful they really are, will their illusions begin to disappear. Even to begin these perceptual changes will awaken something within all, causing each individual to reach beyond the illusionary boundaries they've set for themselves in a search for self-enhancement, not just for their own well-being but for that of the entire village. It has begun. You must now do your part to allow it to continue. Lightly and lovingly pass on your lessons to those seeking growth. All will benefit. You for the intent. Them for the action taken to change. Until then I wish you all, light and happiness.'" When he had finished, Palimar lowered his head in a quiet moment and then raised it back up, moving it from side to side. "I concur," was all he said.

TANDARA'S MANUSCRIPT

GIFTS OF PERCEPTION

THE FIRST TENET

What you really believe. What you hold within your
heart. Will become yours.

Understand your thoughts, for thoughts create your
reality. You end up being what you think you are. You
end up getting what you think you shall. Thoughts are
created by imagination. Imagination is created by the
intentional expansion of mind. And mind is a magic
coupling of all the separate, unique, individual parts
that make up All That Is. You are one of those
wonderful, beautiful, individual separate parts.

Those thoughts, originated and controlled by you, and
then influenced by the energy around you, create your
reality.

THE SECOND TENET

Survival doesn't exist. For all life is ongoing. There is no
easy way. There is no hard way. There just is.

You are Love. Never forget it. Expand and send
yourself out into the world. Be bold enough to share
and influence others with the essence of who your
innerself is. For you are light. You are the word.
You are magic.

THE THIRD TENET

Look to your inner guide to life's answers on your
physical experience. Only by looking within will you begin
to understand the mysteries you've so cleverly
created and have chosen to solve.

Have a conversation with yourself often. Ask yourself
many questions on the specifics of your life. Then
simply remain silent and have the wisdom to listen to
your inner voice. We can guide ourselves through all of
life's obstacles with the knowledge contained within
each of us.

THE FOURTH TENET

Never doubt yourself or your own power.

Life is a series of events that we bring into our world for the experience. There are always rewards for our efforts.

THE FIFTH TENET

Growth comes by way of allowance of another
person's touch.

Each experience begins an unending spiral throughout
eternity of repeated experiences until the lesson is
learned. Only then will the circle be closed to allow room
for new growth and additional advancement.

THE SIXTH TENET

Your eyes are an aspect of your physicality. Your
intuitive awareness an aspect of your spirituality. When
in direct competition for your perception, allow your
inner light to be your guide.

With each passing moment we effect our eternal mark
on each other. As such, we move forward or backward,
depending upon our alignment to truth. View each
encounter in a positive light, and all energy sent by you
toward another will forge an endearing bond.

THE SEVENTH TENET

Sometimes a straight line between your initial thought
and its ultimate goal is not the fastest route to
creation.

Give thought to the interruptions throughout your
daily life. Accidents, no. Mistakes, no. Planned
encounters, yes. Brought together through mutually
magnetized energy on a neutral basis to enhance the
creative process.

THE EIGHTH TENET

The stepping stone to creation is action.
Without it, all thought will dwindle and die.

Fire your thoughts with passion, which by its very
nature requires movement. Stagnation will
not allow you your goal. Only a steady stream
of motion. Any kind of motion.
For even if the wrong fork in the road is chosen,
corrections cannot be made if
forward movement hasn't begun.

Jeff Gutterman

THE NINTH TENET

If you choose positive projections for your
thought patterns,
you will continually surround yourself within an
attitude of Love.

Focus on yourself and your future.
Choose wisely to make it right for you,
and then allow the flow of energy from your center
to spread outward, moving you forward, seducing
others to sense and gather your strength,
thereby enhancing their own.

THE TENTH TENET

Sense what's in your heart as the truth. Everything
else is an illusion.

Intellect is a wonderful part of your physical
experience, but should never guide you into something
if your inner feelings are to move you away from it.
Trust only what you sense deep down inside yourself,
for your chosen path is filled with many illusionary
perceptions. Growth comes about by moving
through these deceptions and around the imaginary
barriers you've allowed them to create.

THE FINAL TENET

Life. Physical. Nonphysical. Is a game. The only reality
behind it is that of Thought, Creation, and Movement.
Life is about changes. Nothing stays the same.

All that you see before you doesn't really exist,
except in your mind where all things are possible.
Pull toward you the visions you wish to experience
and reject those that you do not. If you are wholly
yourself, you can only magnetize those things to you
that are truth and thereafter positive experiences.
Anything else entering the world of your mind, means
you are not being who you really are in all
circumstances, and therefore by your own initiation,
you hold back the light of love from your true being.
Strive always to be uplifting and positive.
Strive always to be you.

On the author and the publishing company

For a writing career that began by writing lyrics with a well-known pop singer back in the mid 1960s, the author has managed to put pen to paper in a variety of mediums for nearly thirty years now. Born and raised in the Los Angeles area, he maintains his home in the suburbs with his illusionary golden retriever, Dakota, and continues his nearly three decade stint as both a student and teacher of parapsychological thought. His formal education and degrees come from almost nine years in both the Texas and California University systems, and claims travels that have allowed him an enjoyable landscape and diversification of people, not only throughout this country, but also into certain areas of Canada, Mexico, and Costa Rica. He prides himself on making new friends easily and puts the length of some of his friendships at over forty years.

SilverWind Publishing was formed in 1998 to produce works of fiction & nonfiction in both the written and audio forms, that in some way may lend a hand in encouraging awareness & stimulating growth.

Take a moment and look toward the stars,
And imagine
Imagine your true essence
That inner core of who you really are,
Shining just as brightly.
Held in your world by invisible hands
In a space that shares itself
With other stars
Whose true essence is also light.